BANANA FOX AND THE GUMMY MONSTER MESS

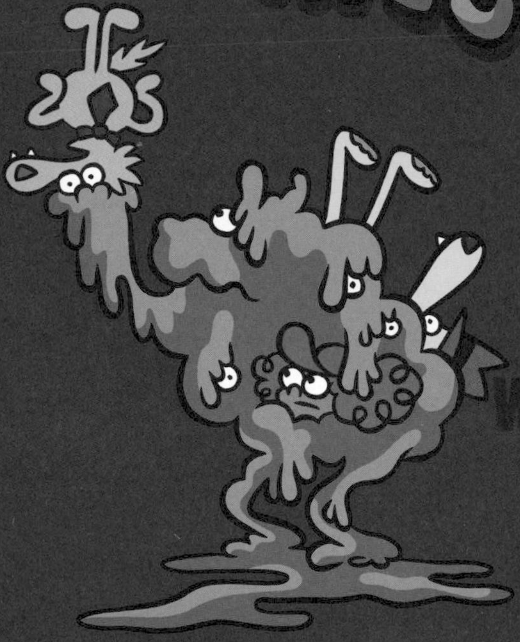

A GRAPHIC NOVEL BY

JAMES KOCHALKA

graphix
An Imprint of
SCHOLASTIC

For Aunt Margy

Copyright © 2022 by James Kochalka

All rights reserved. Published by Graphix, an imprint of Scholastic Inc., *Publishers since 1920*. SCHOLASTIC, GRAPHIX, and associated logos are trademarks and/or registered trademarks of Scholastic Inc.

Library of Congress Control Number: 2021937767

ISBN 978-1-338-66055-5 (hardcover)
ISBN 978-1-338-66054-8 (paperback)

10 9 8 7 6 5 4 3 2 1   22 23 24 25 26

Printed in China   62
First edition, May 2022

Edited by Megan Peace
Book design by Steve Ponzo
Creative Director: Phil Falco
Publisher: David Saylor

CONTENTS

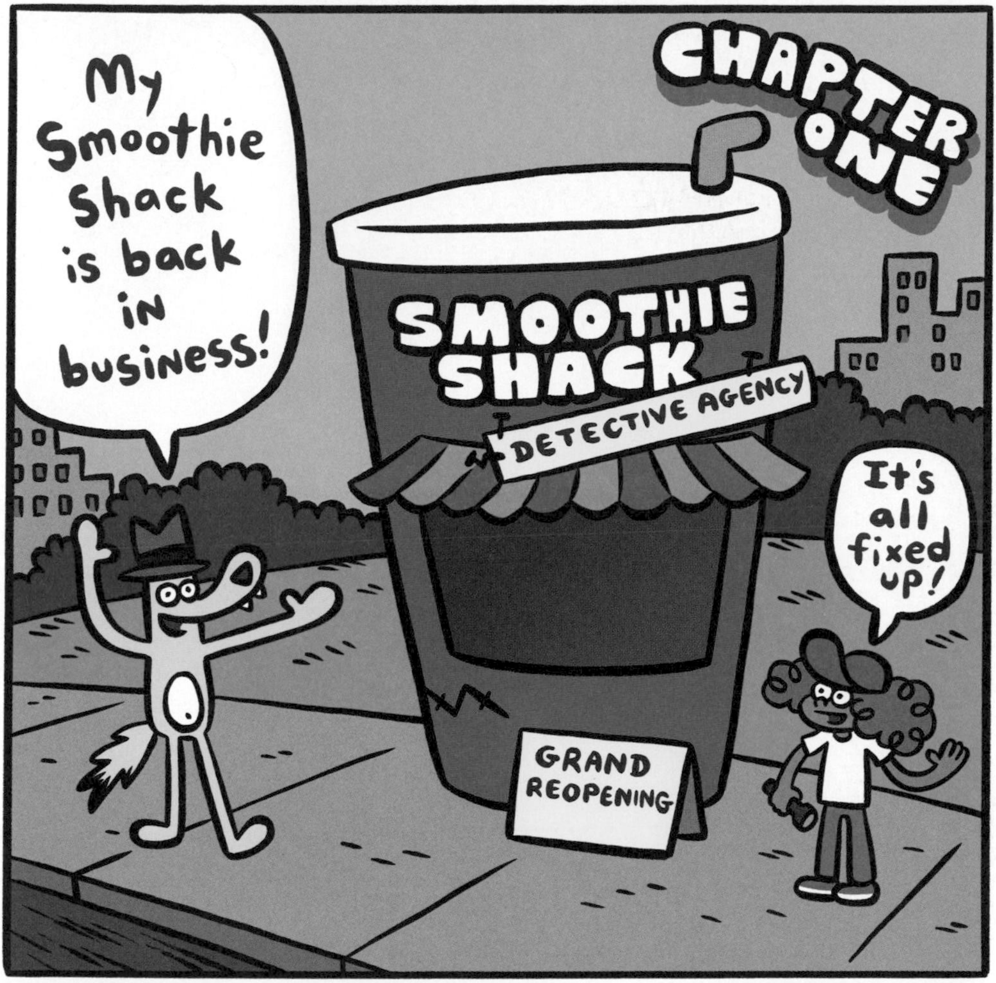
CHAPTER ONE
My Smoothie Shack is back in business!
SMOOTHIE SHACK
DETECTIVE AGENCY
It's all fixed up!
GRAND REOPENING

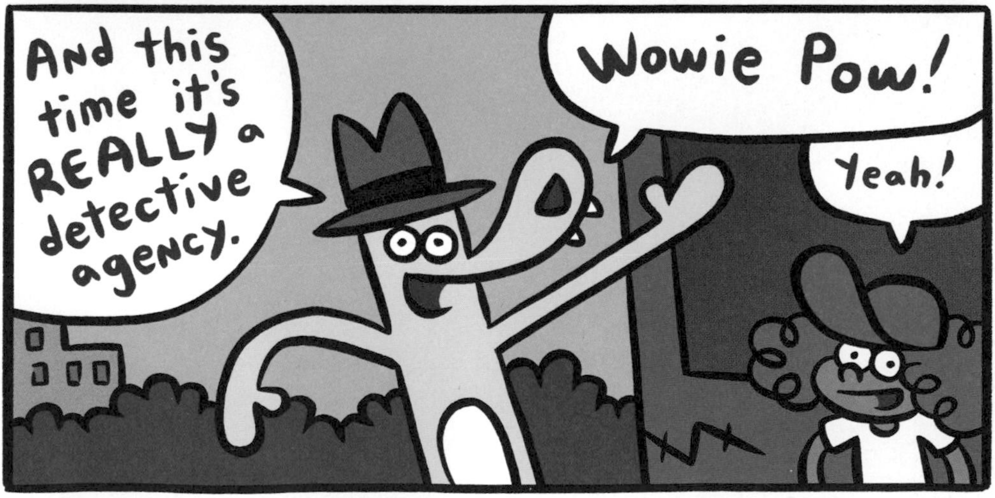
And this time it's REALLY a detective agency.
Wowie Pow!
Yeah!

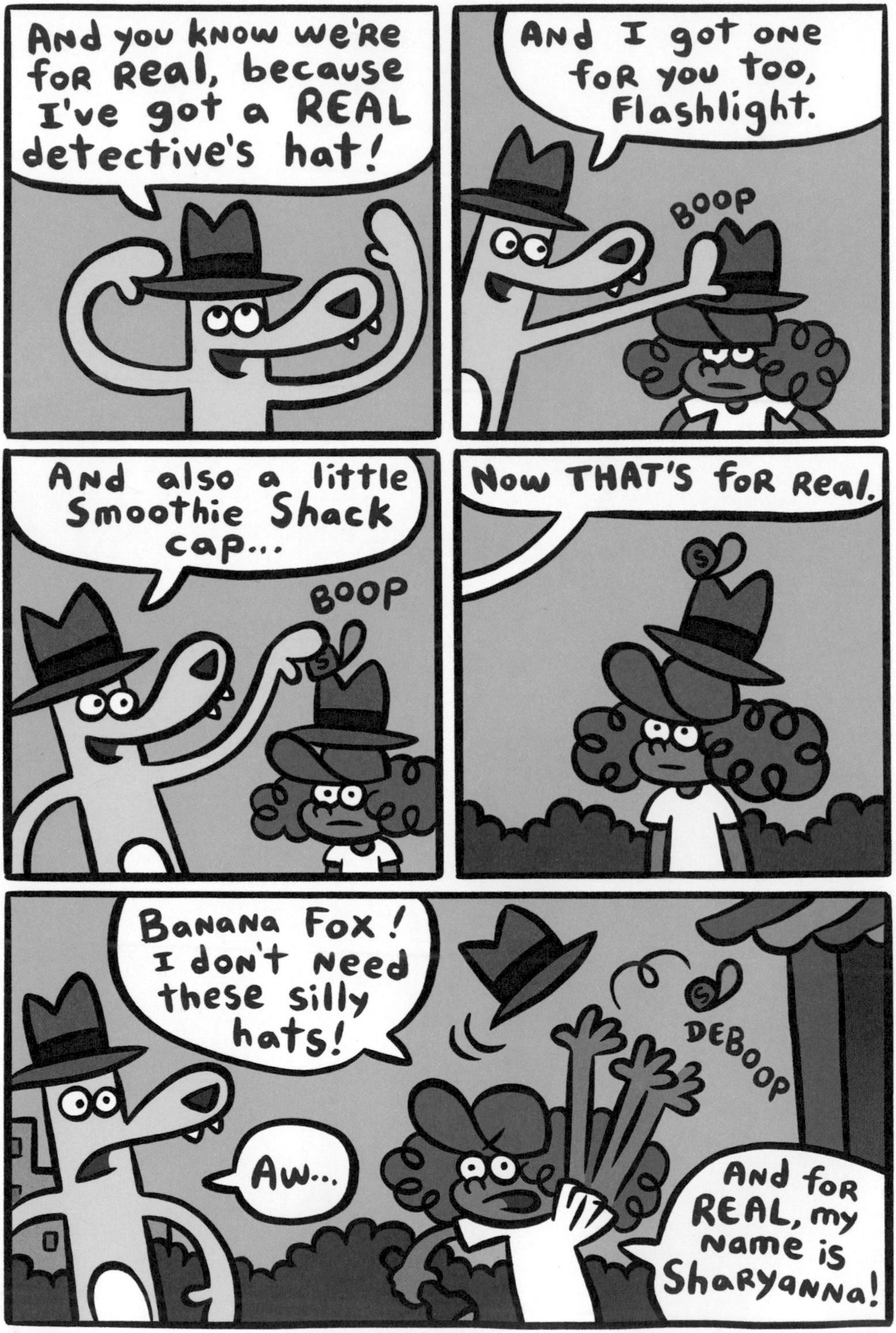
And you know we're for Real, because I've got a REAL detective's hat!
And I got one for you too, Flashlight.
BOOP
And also a little Smoothie Shack cap...
BOOP
Now THAT'S for Real.
Banana Fox! I don't need these silly hats!
DEBOOP
Aw...
And for REAL, my name is Sharyanna!

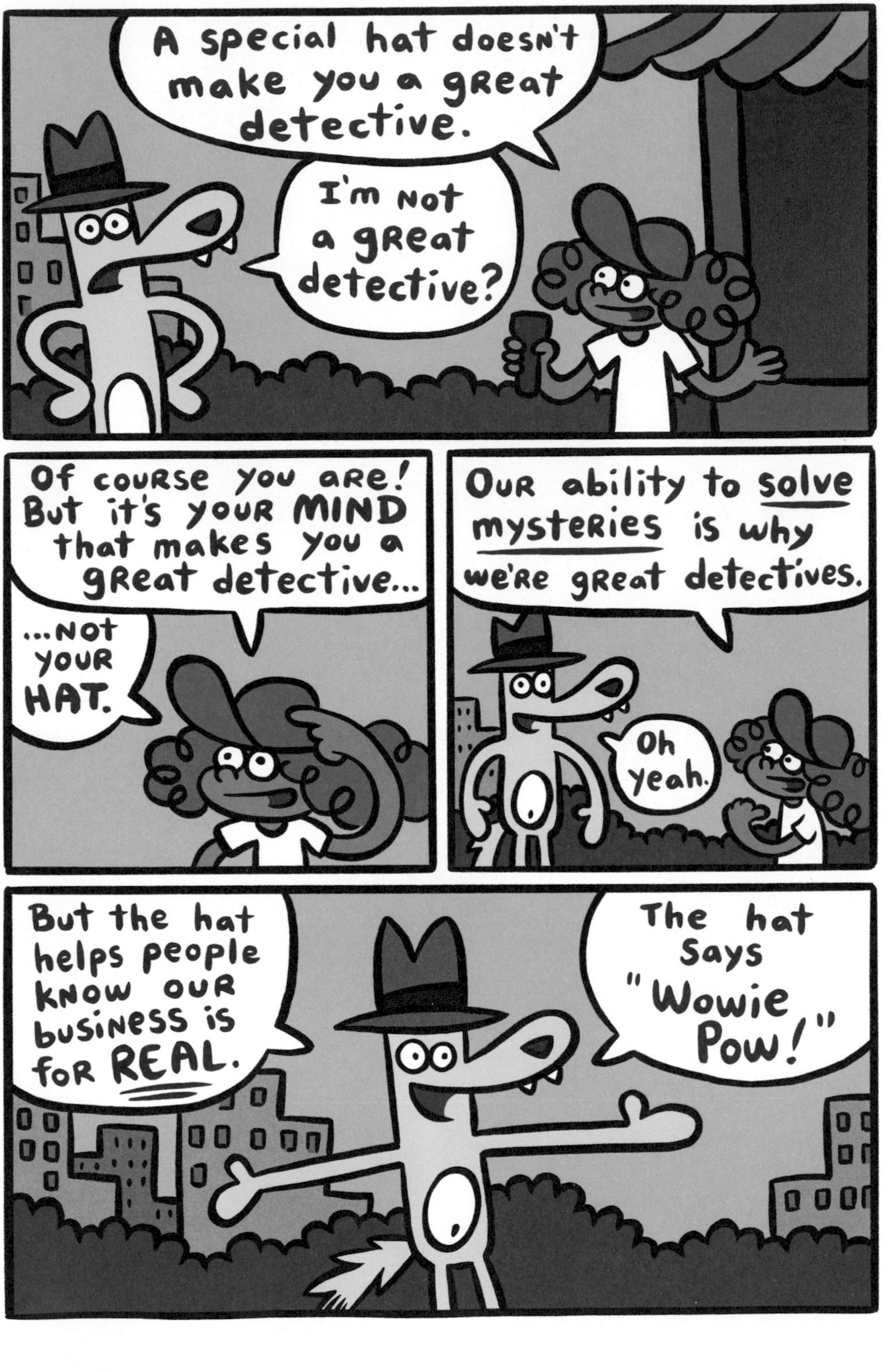
A special hat doesn't make you a great detective.
I'm not a great detective?
Of course you are! But it's your MIND that makes you a great detective...
...not your HAT.
Our ability to solve mysteries is why we're great detectives.
Oh yeah.
But the hat helps people know our business is for REAL.
The hat says "Wowie Pow!"

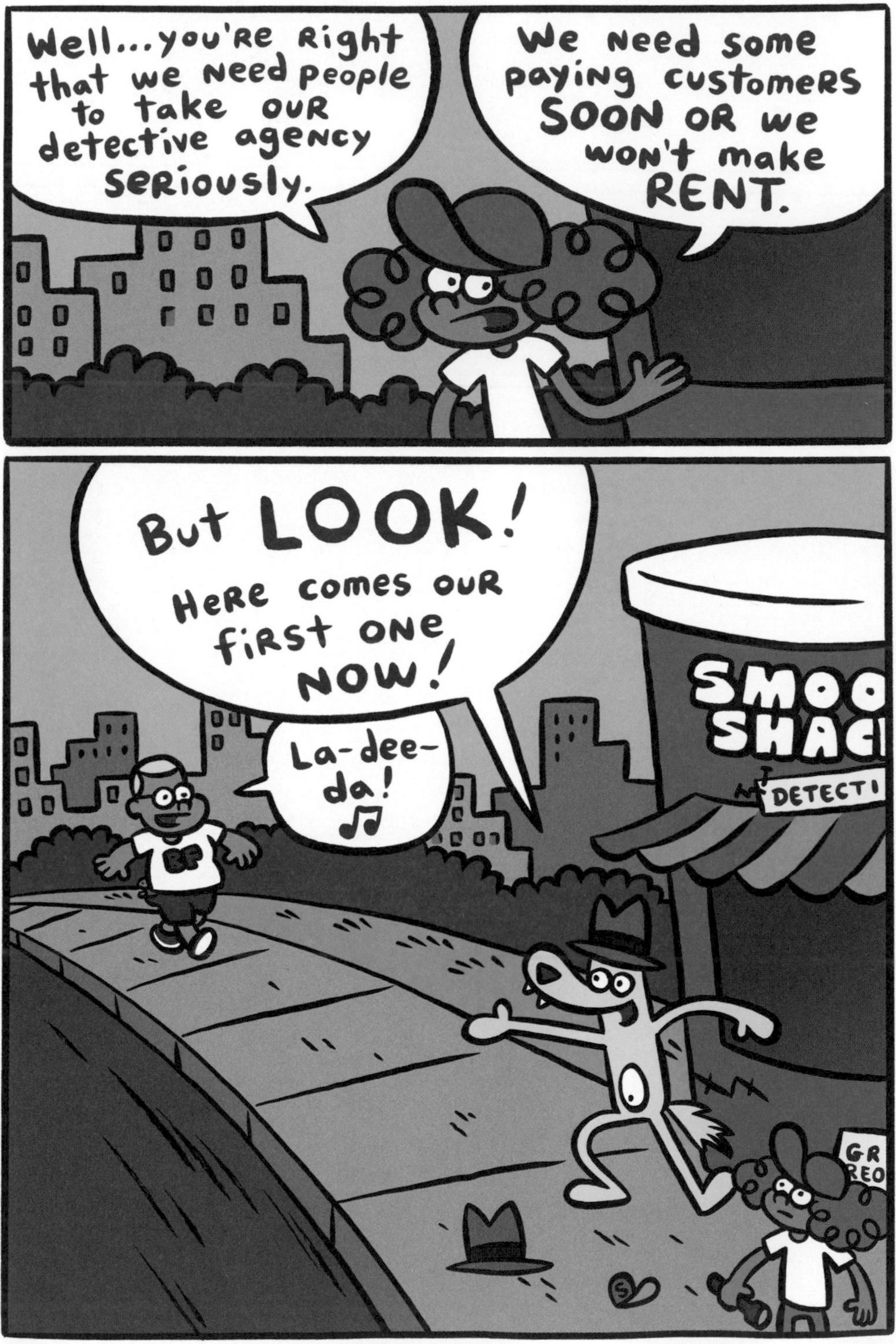
Well... you're right that we need people to take our detective agency seriously.
We need some paying customers SOON or we won't make RENT.
But LOOK! Here comes our first one NOW!
La-dee-da! ♫
SMOO
SHAC
DETECTI
GR
REO

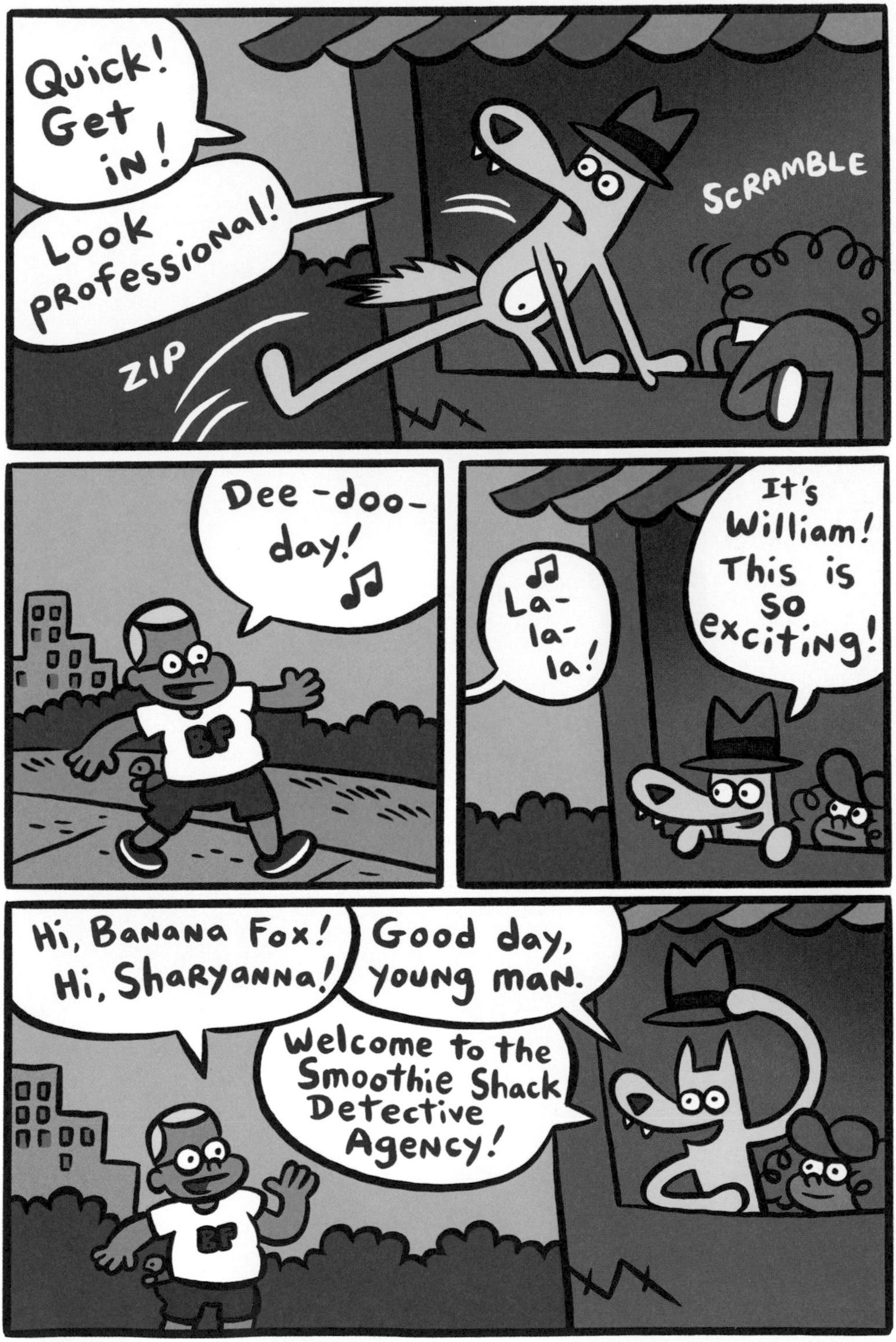
Quick! Get in!
Look professional!
SCRAMBLE
ZIP
Dee-doo-day!
La-la-la!
It's William! This is so exciting!
Hi, Banana Fox! Hi, Sharyanna!
Good day, young man.
Welcome to the Smoothie Shack Detective Agency!

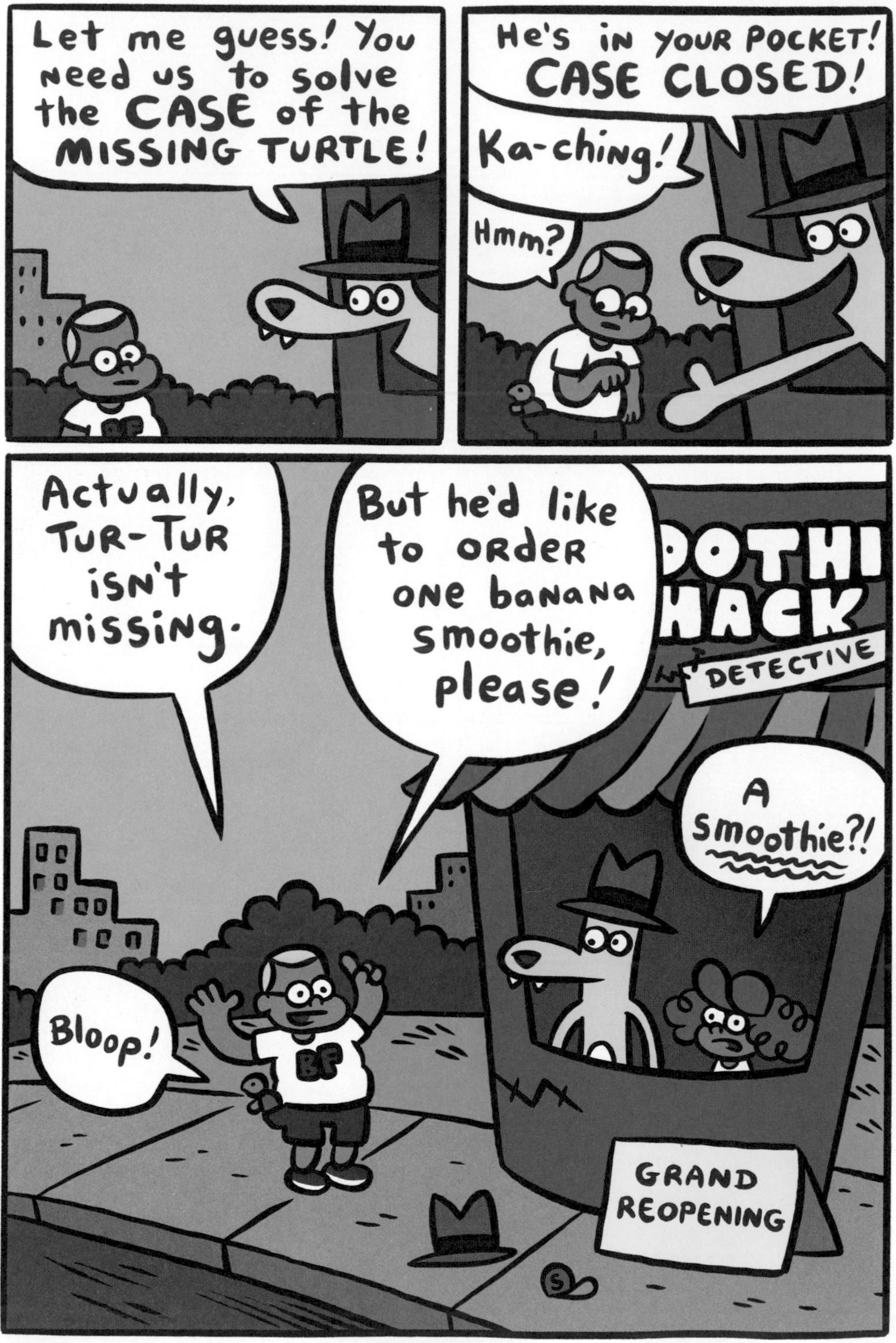
Let me guess! You need us to solve the CASE of the MISSING TURTLE!
He's in your POCKET! CASE CLOSED!
Ka-ching!
Hmm?
Actually, TUR-TUR isn't missing.
But he'd like to order one banana smoothie, please!
DETECTIVE
A smoothie?!
Bloop!
GRAND REOPENING

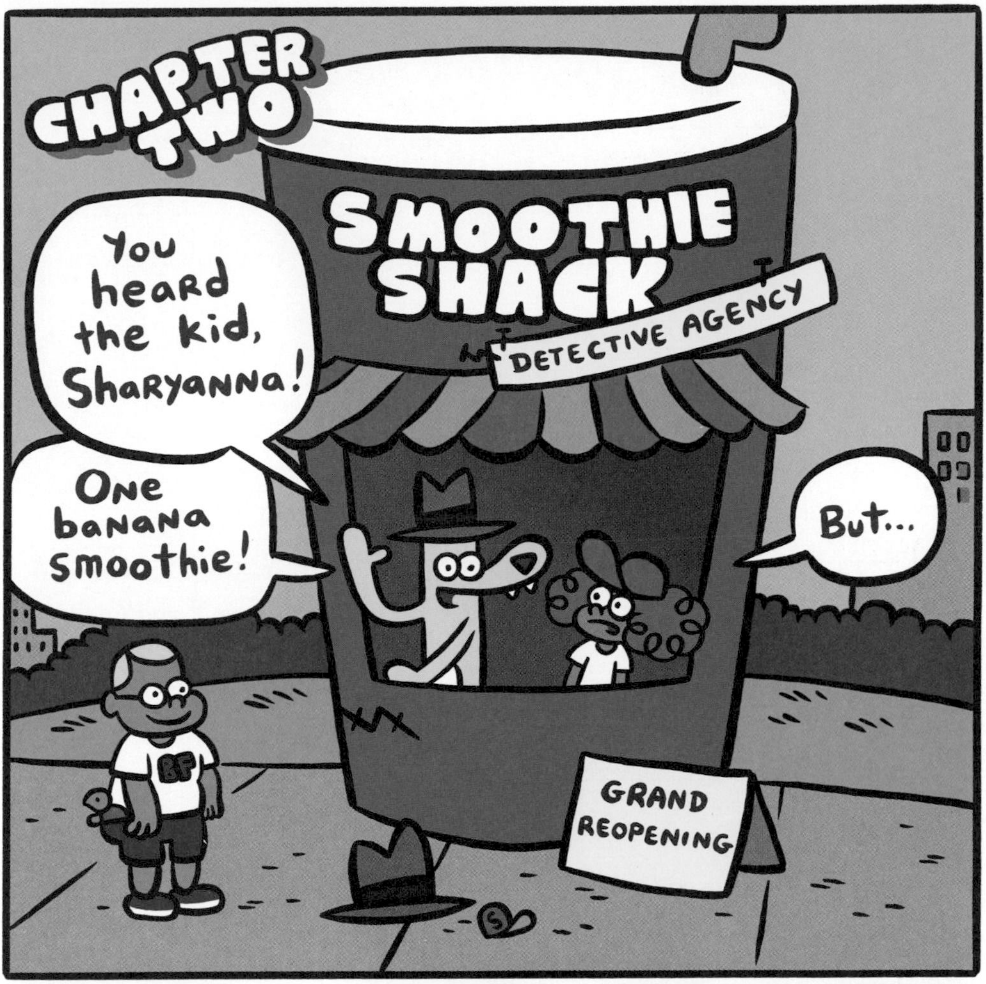
CHAPTER TWO
SMOOTHIE SHACK
DETECTIVE AGENCY
You heard the kid, Sharyanna!
One banana smoothie!
But...
GRAND REOPENING

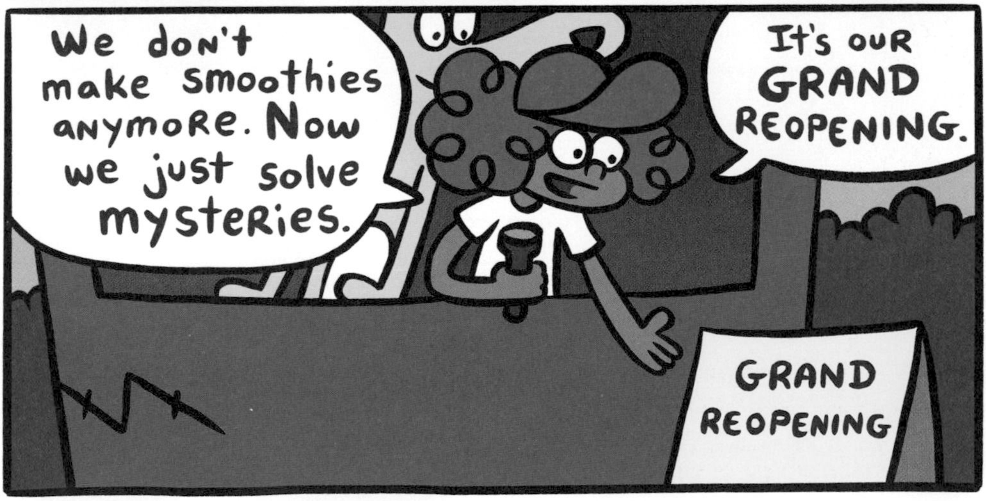
We don't make smoothies anymore. Now we just solve mysteries.
It's our GRAND REOPENING.
GRAND REOPENING

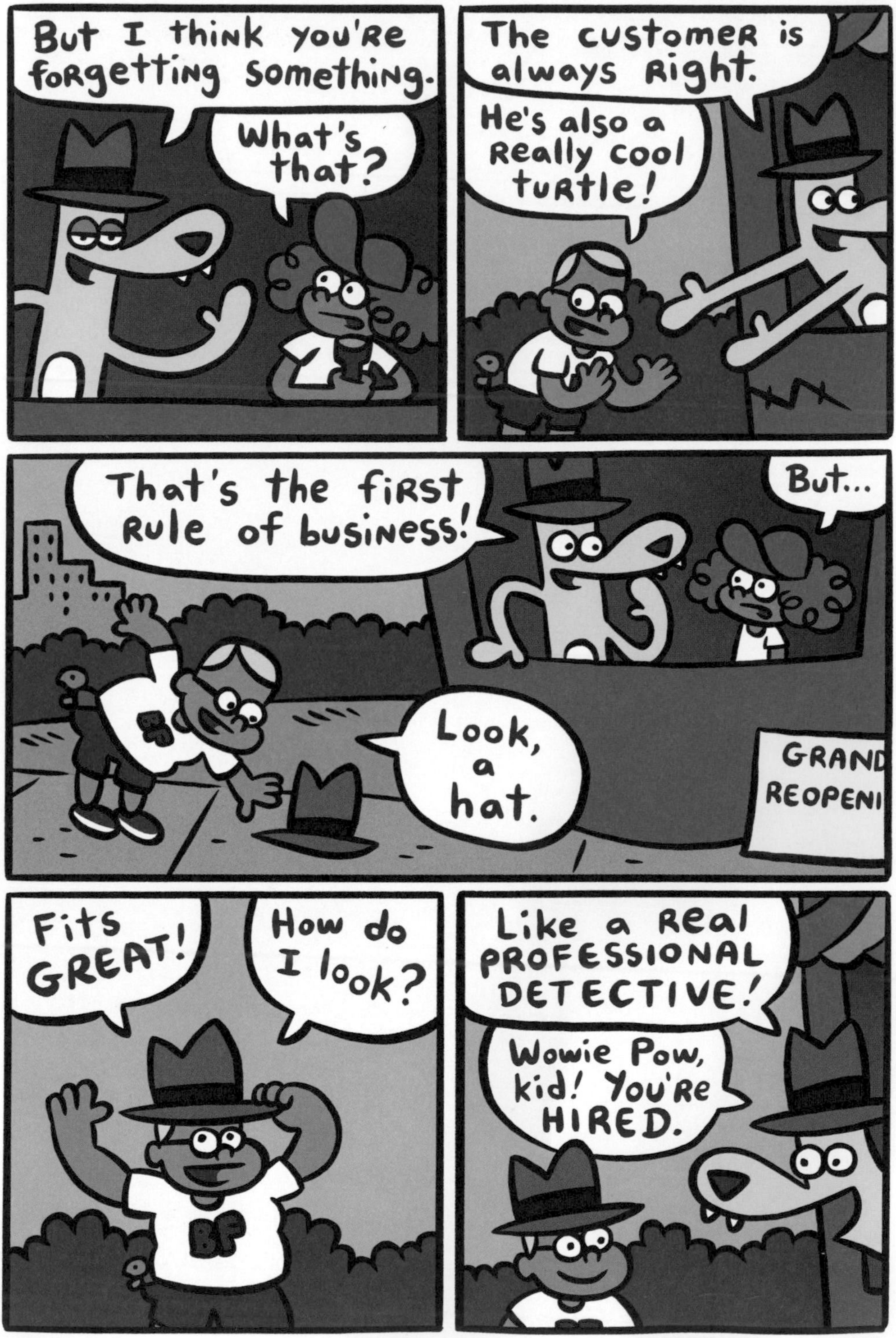
But I think you're forgetting something.
What's that?
The customer is always right.
He's also a really cool turtle!
That's the first rule of business!
But...
Look, a hat.
GRAND
REOPENI
Fits GREAT!
How do I look?
Like a real PROFESSIONAL DETECTIVE!
Wowie Pow, kid! You're HIRED.

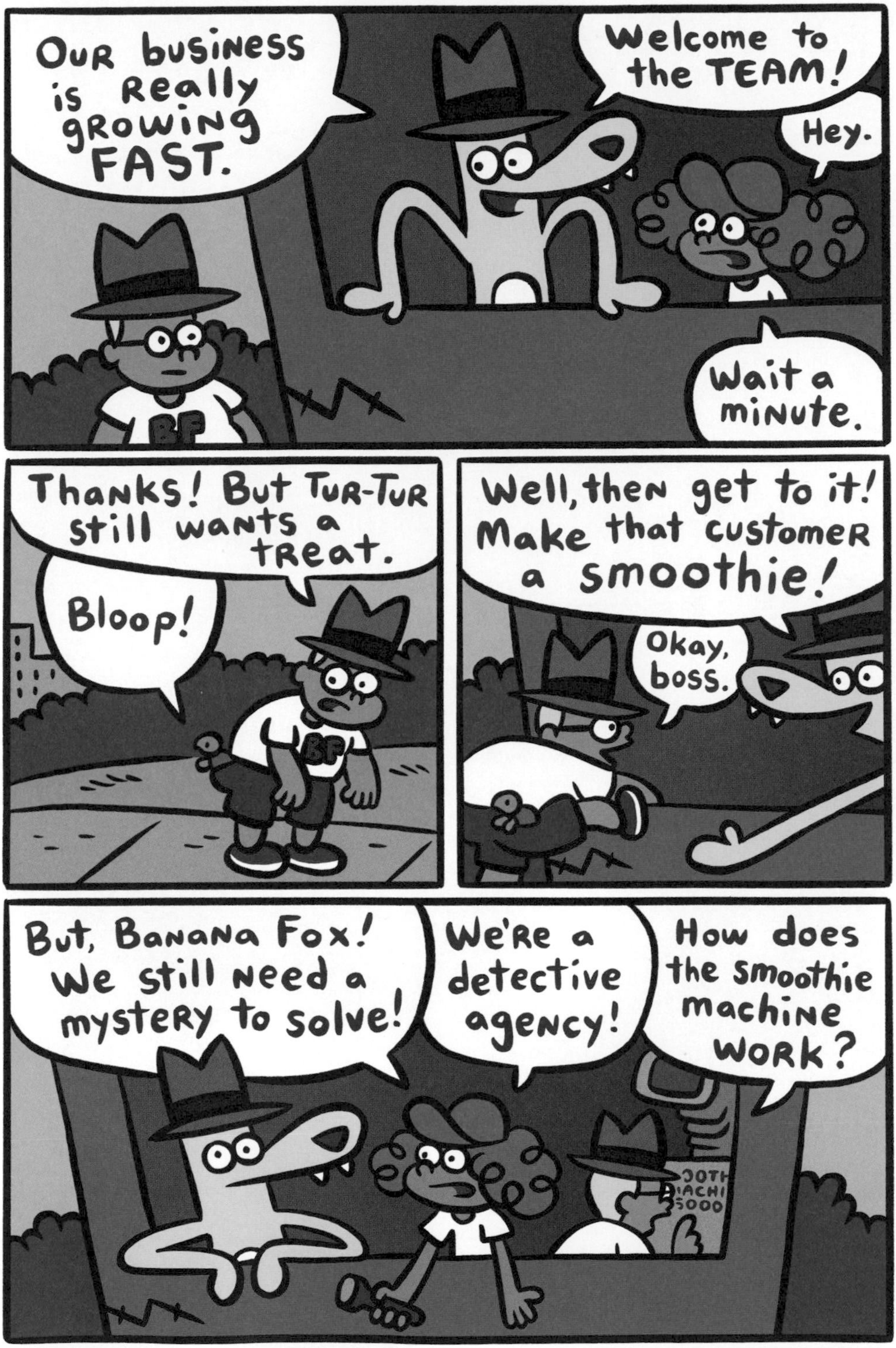
Our business is Really growing FAST.
Welcome to the TEAM!
Hey.
Wait a minute.
Thanks! But TUR-TUR still wants a treat.
Bloop!
Well, then get to it! Make that customer a smoothie!
Okay, boss.
But, Banana Fox! We still need a mystery to solve!
We're a detective agency!
How does the smoothie machine WORK?

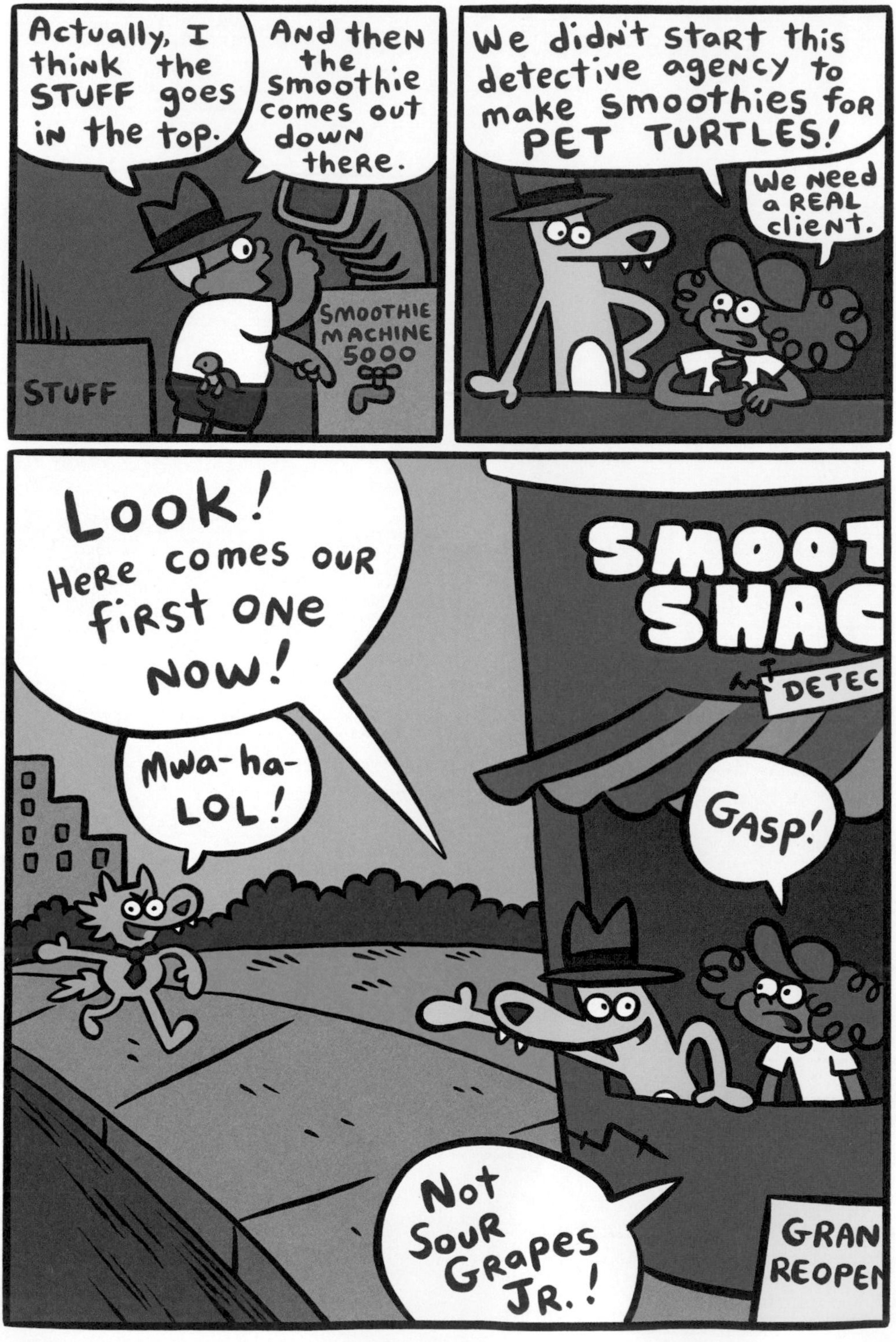
Actually, I think the STUFF goes in the top.
And then the smoothie comes out down there.
STUFF
SMOOTHIE MACHINE 5000
We didn't start this detective agency to make smoothies for PET TURTLES!
We need a REAL client.
LOOK! Here comes our first one now!
SMOOT
SHAC
DETEC
Mwa-ha-LOL!
GASP!
Not Sour Grapes Jr.!
GRAN
REOPEN

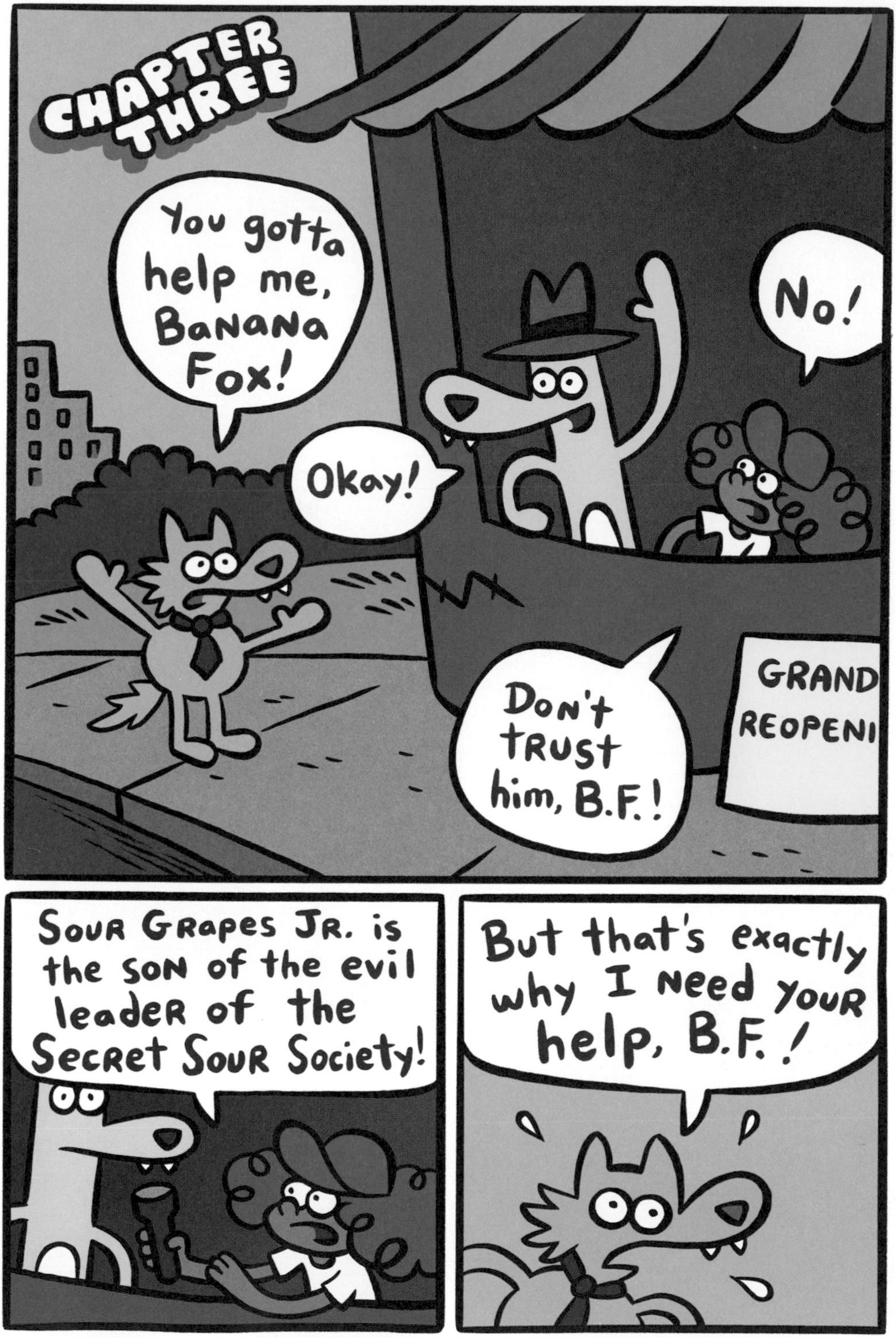
CHAPTER THREE
You gotta help me, Banana Fox!
Okay!
No!
GRAND REOPENI
Don't TRUST him, B.F.!
Sour Grapes Jr. is the son of the evil leader of the Secret Sour Society!
But that's exactly why I need your help, B.F.!

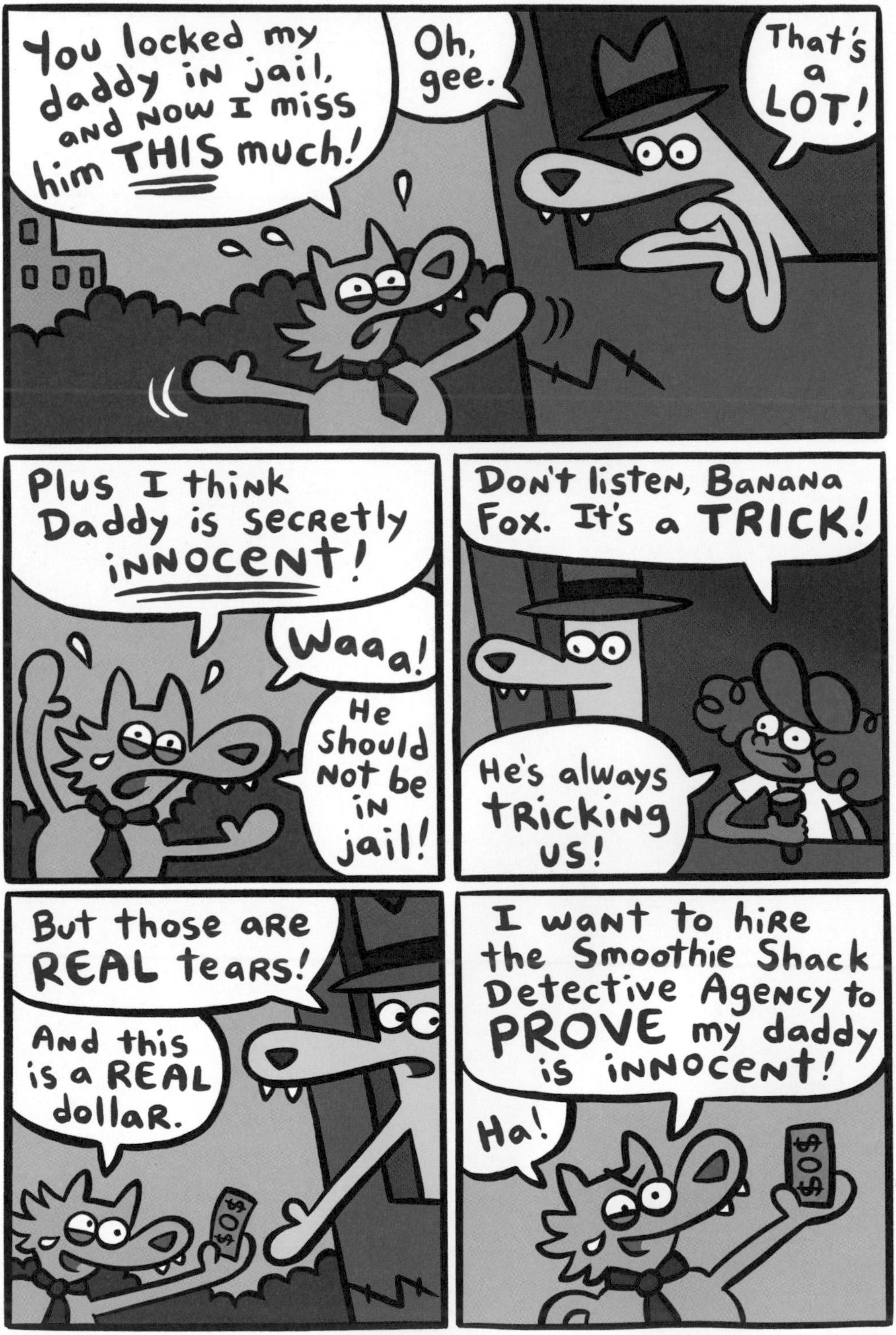
You locked my daddy in jail, and now I miss him THIS much!
Oh, gee.
That's a LOT!
Plus I think Daddy is secretly INNOCENT!
Waaa!
He should not be in jail!
Don't listen, Banana Fox. It's a TRICK!
He's always TRICKING US!
But those are REAL tears!
And this is a REAL dollar.
I want to hire the Smoothie Shack Detective Agency to PROVE my daddy is innocent!
Ha!

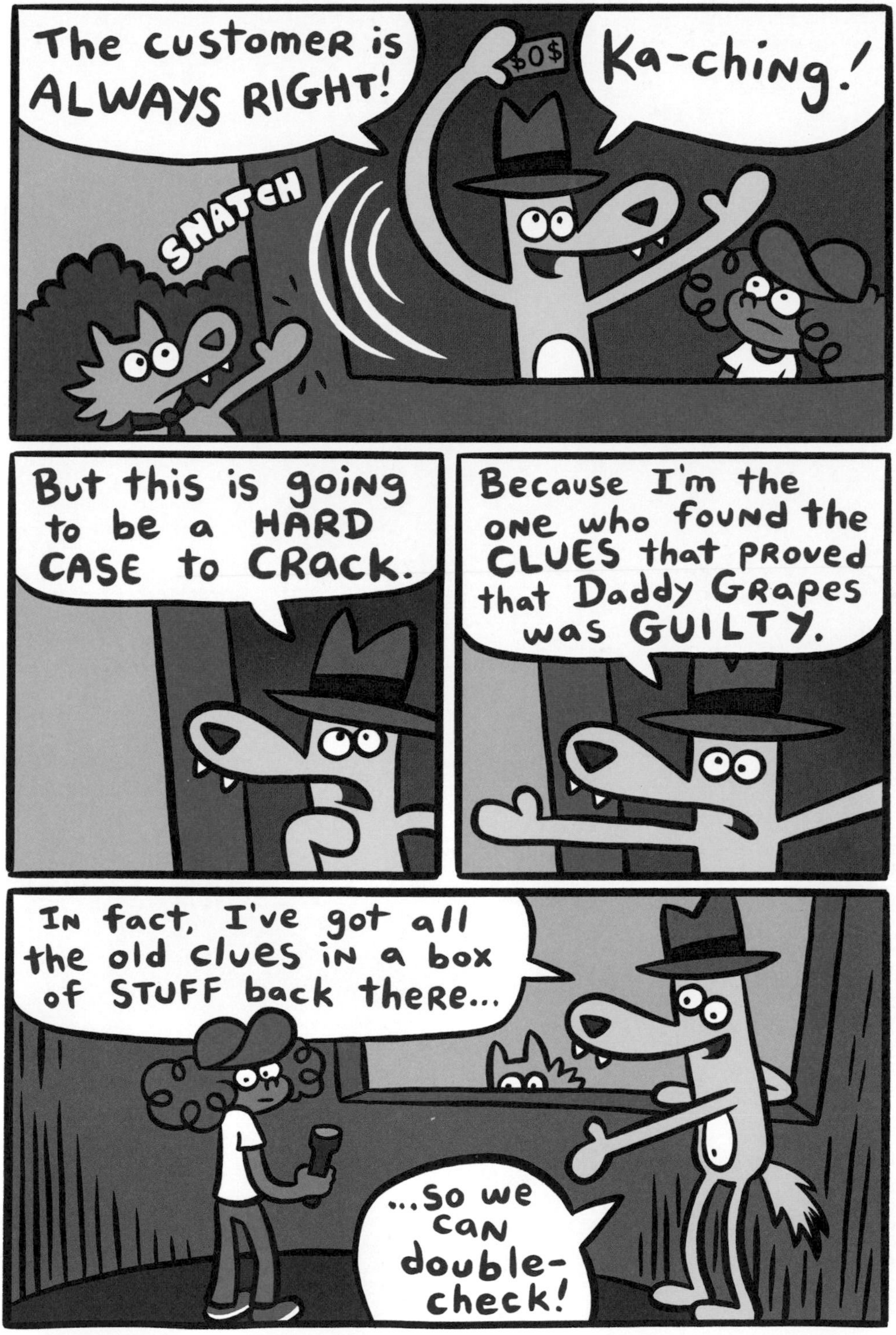
The customer is ALWAYS RIGHT!
0
Ka-ching!
SNATCH
But this is going to be a HARD CASE to CRack.
Because I'm the one who found the CLUES that proved that Daddy Grapes was GUILTY.
In fact, I've got all the old clues in a box of STUFF back there...
...so we can double-check!

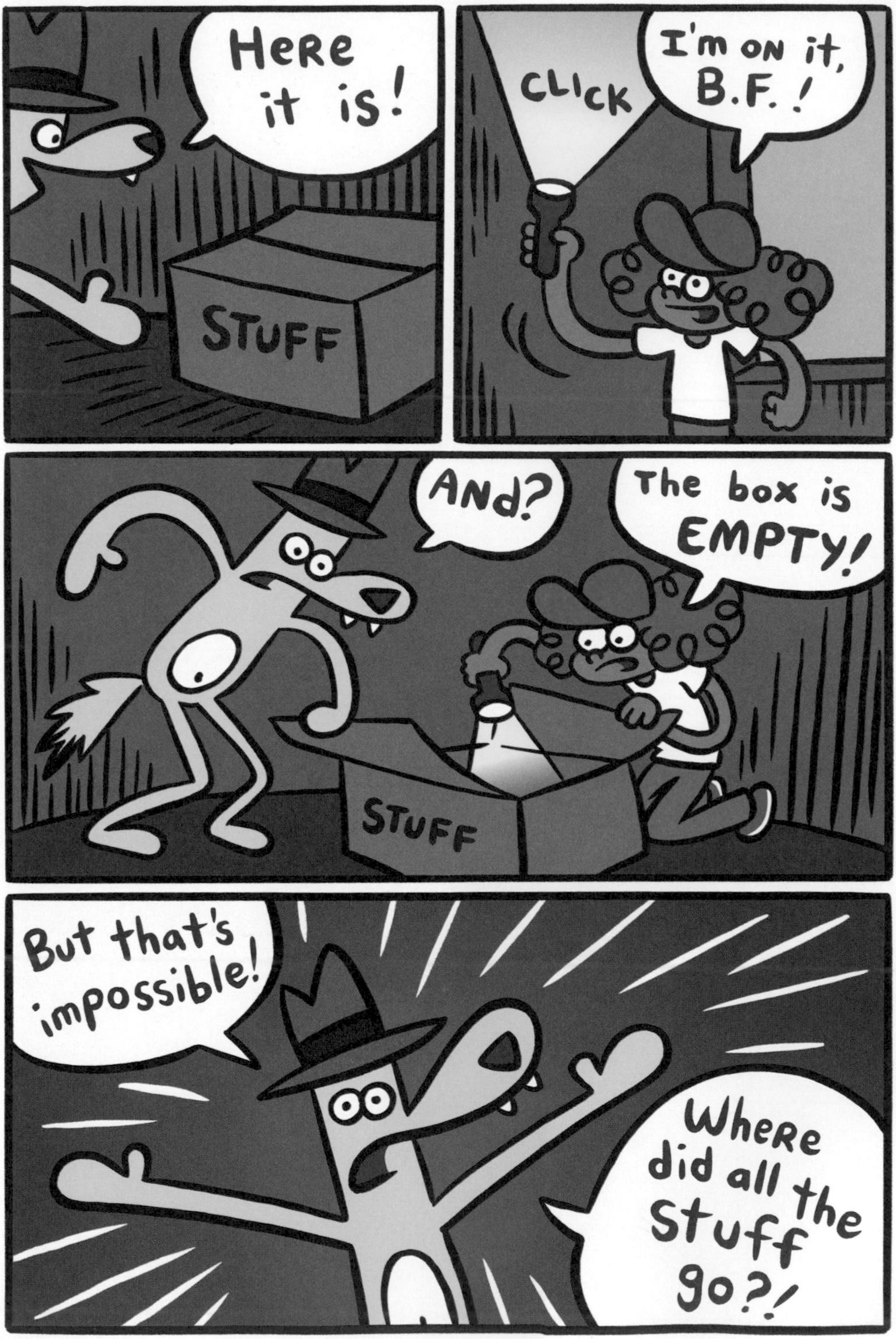
Here it is!
STUFF
CLICK
I'm on it, B.F.!
AND?
The box is EMPTY!
STUFF
But that's impossible!
Where did all the stuff go?!

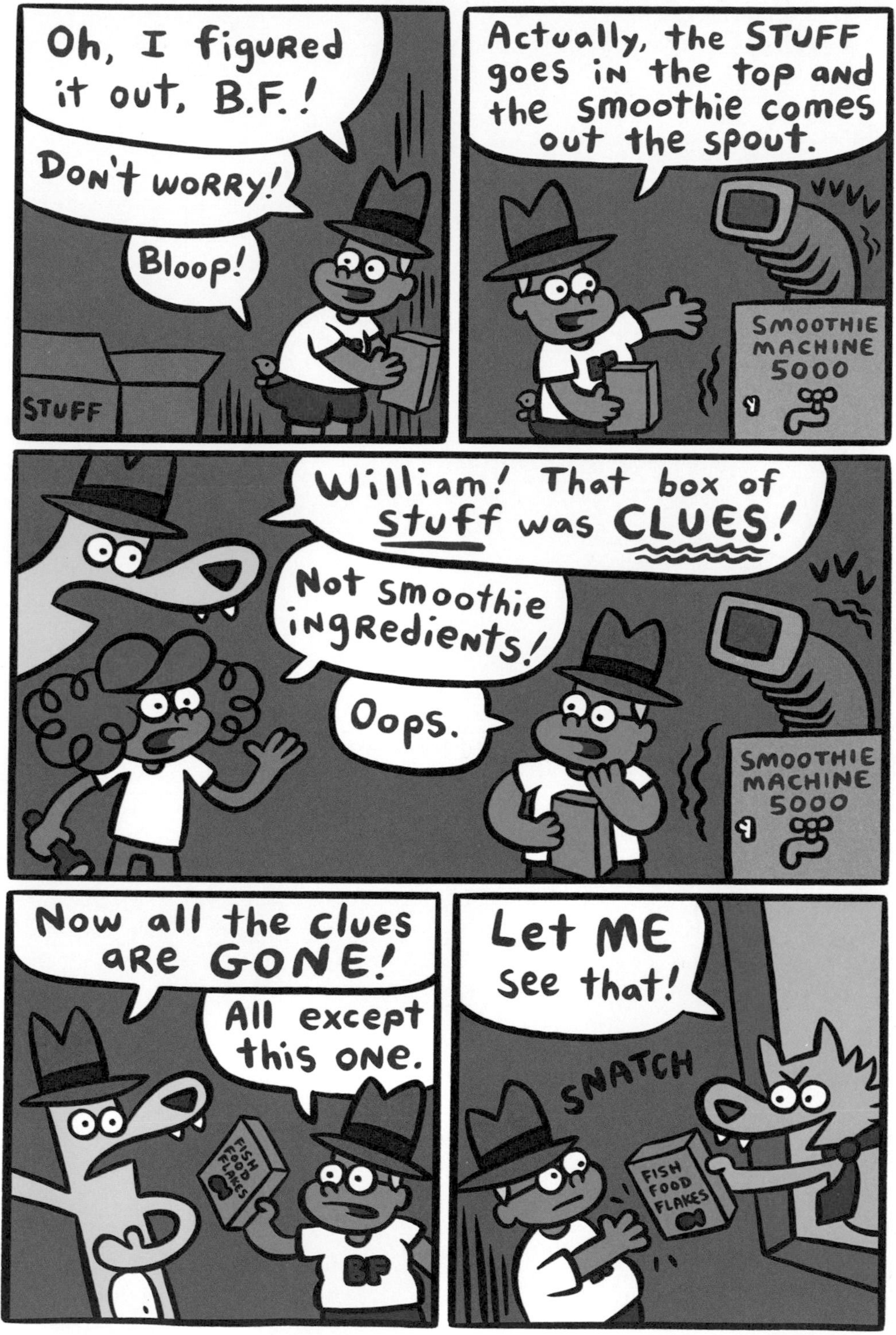
Oh, I figured it out, B.F.!
Don't worry!
Bloop!
STUFF
Actually, the STUFF goes in the top and the smoothie comes out the spout.
SMOOTHIE MACHINE 5000
William! That box of stuff was CLUES!
Not smoothie ingredients!
Oops.
SMOOTHIE MACHINE 5000
Now all the clues are GONE!
All except this one.
FISH FOOD FLAKES
BF
Let ME see that!
SNATCH
FISH FOOD FLAKES

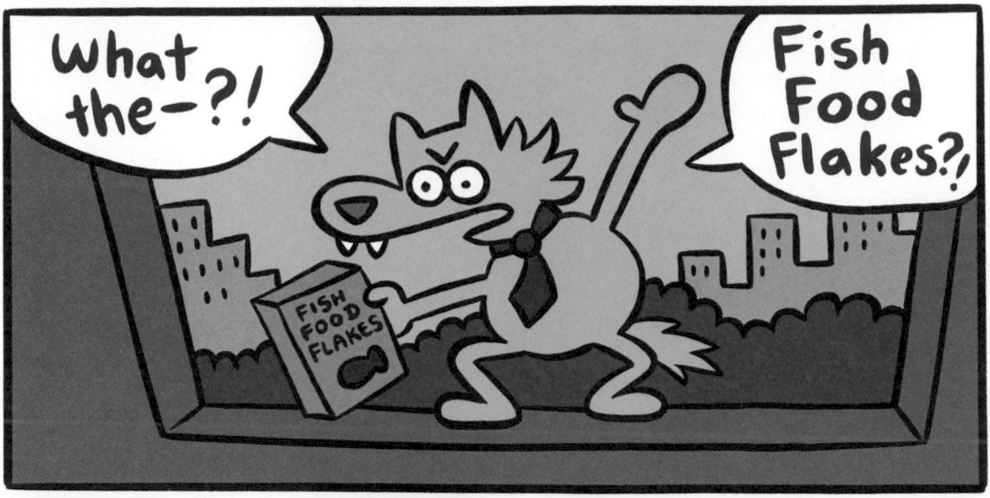
What the-?!
Fish Food Flakes?!
FISH FOOD FLAKES

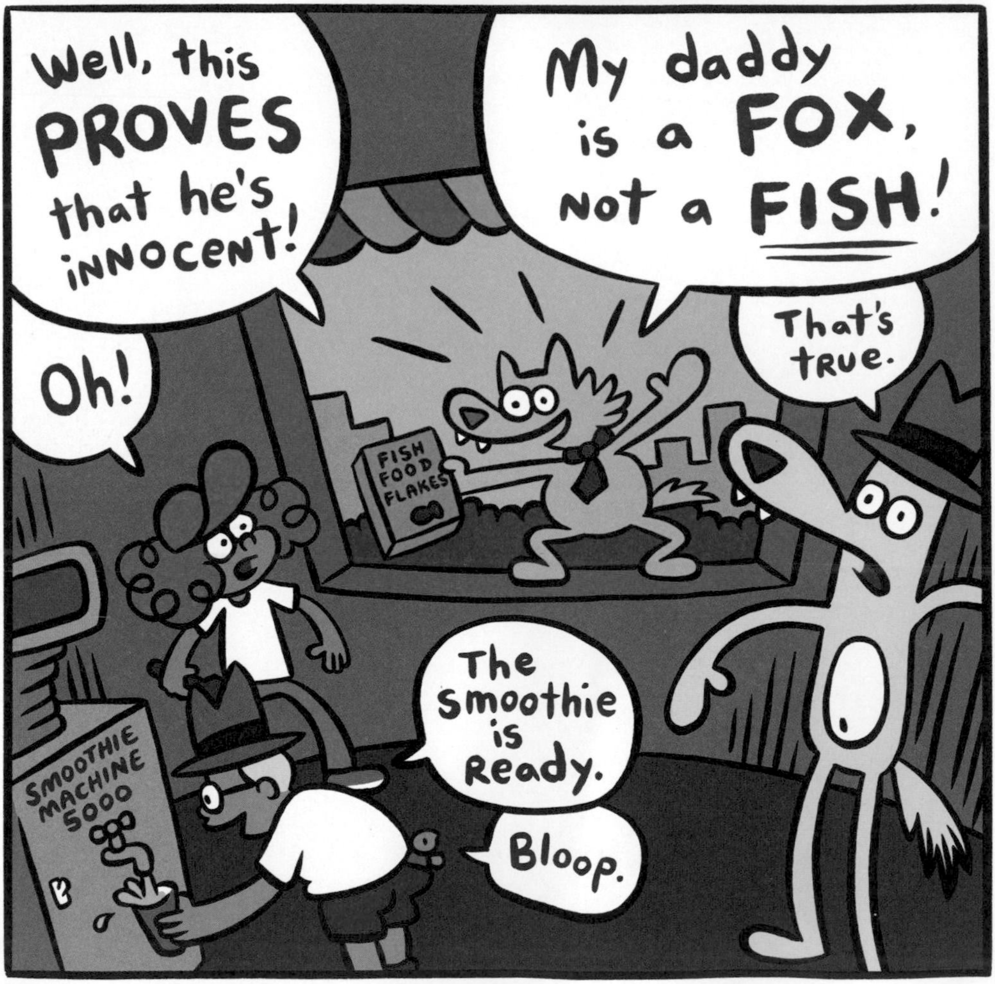
Well, this PROVES that he's innocent!
My daddy is a FOX, not a FISH!
Oh!
That's true.
FISH FOOD FLAKES
The smoothie is Ready.
SMOOTHIE MACHINE 5000
Bloop.

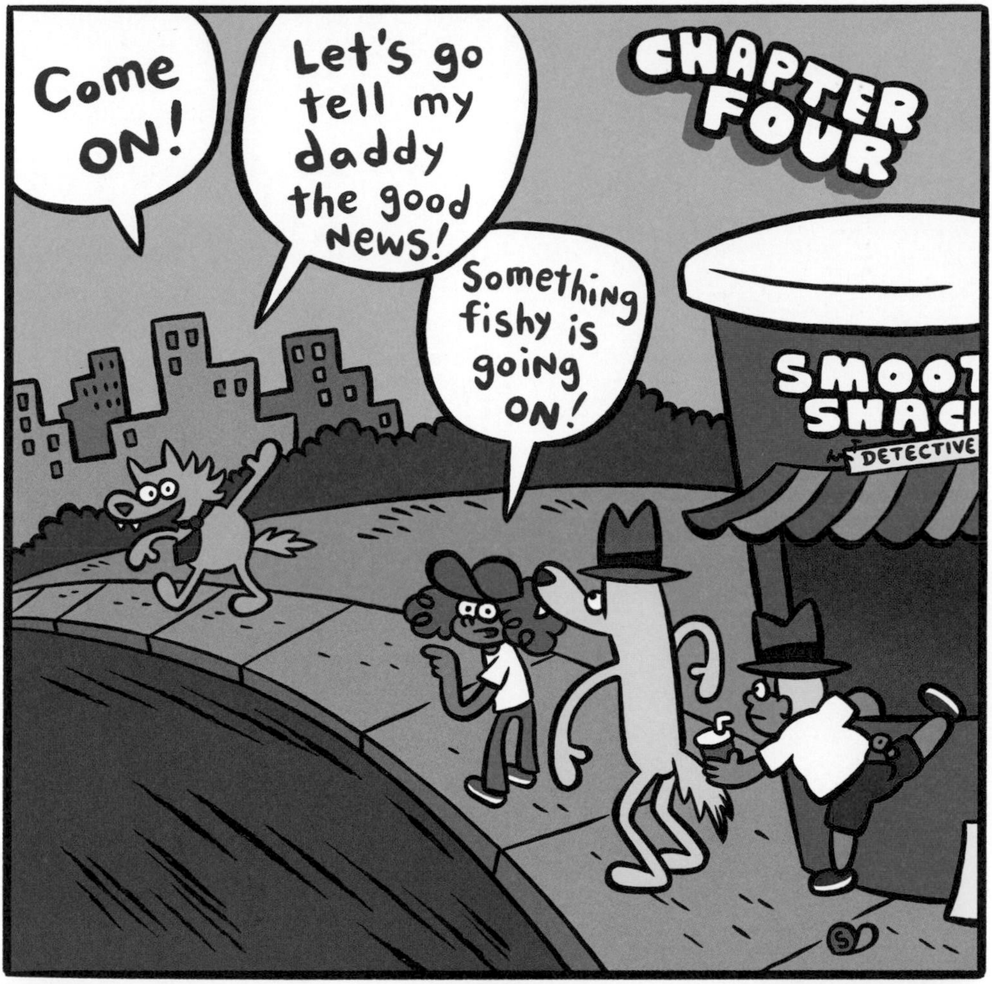
CHAPTER FOUR
Come ON!
Let's go tell my daddy the good NEWS!
Something fishy is going ON!
SMOOT
SHAC
DETECTIVE
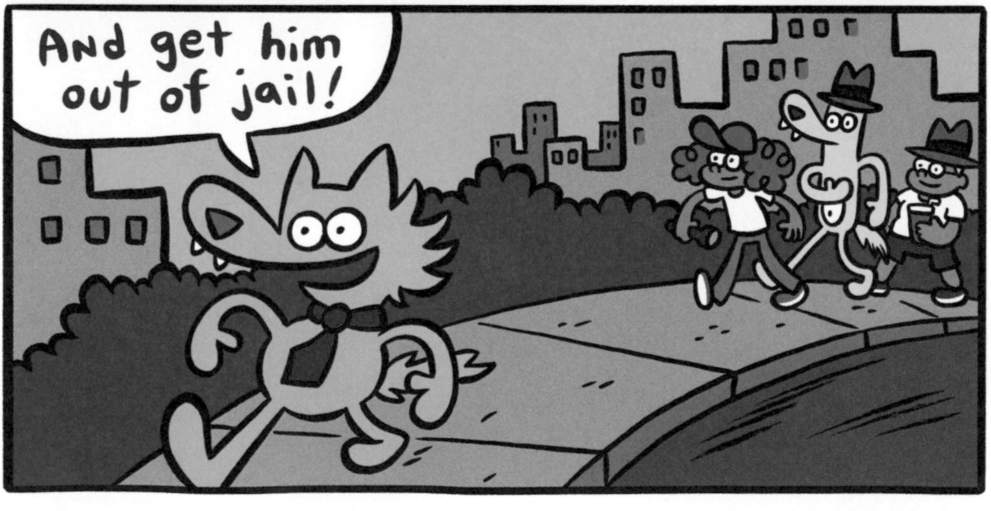
And get him out of jail!

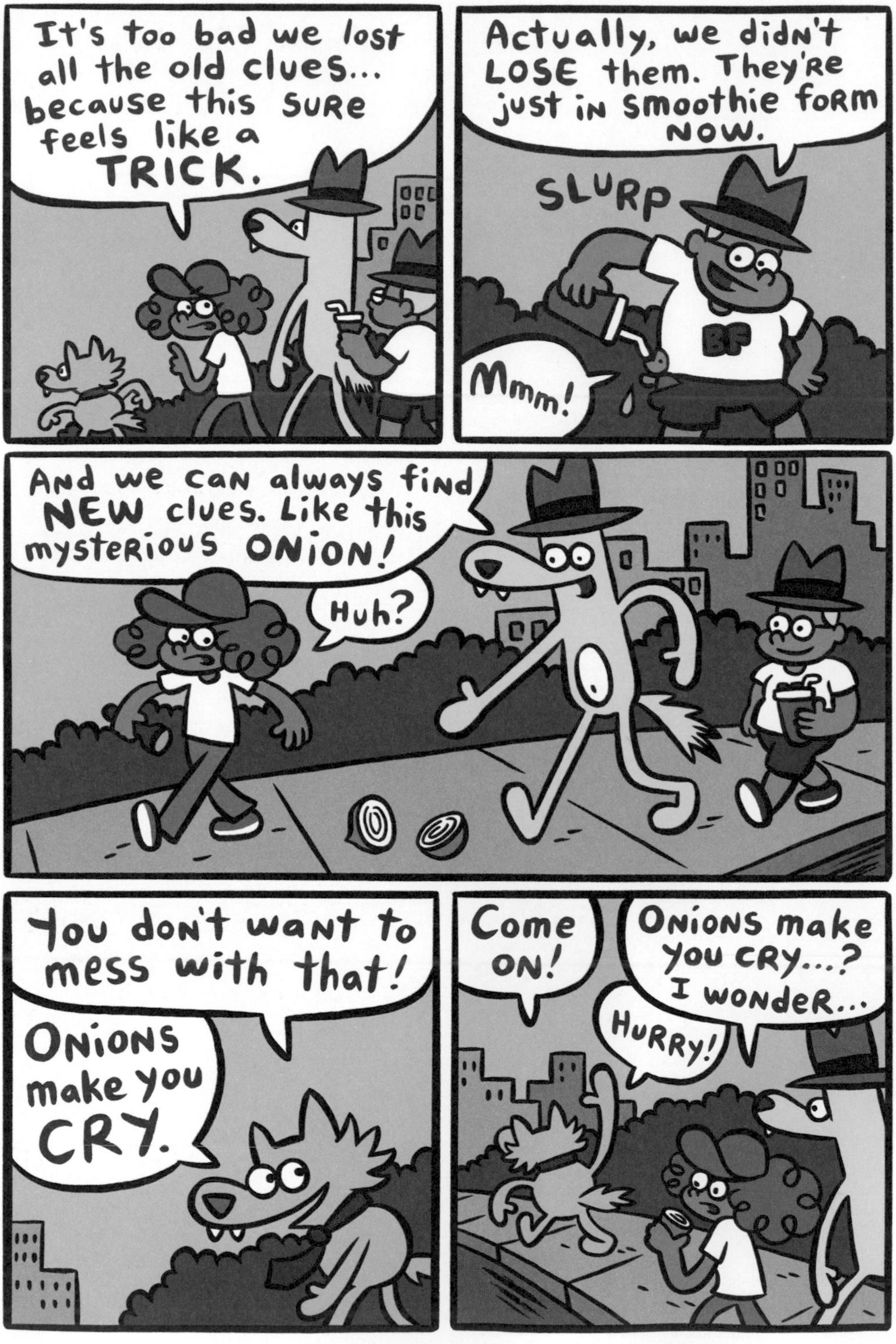
It's too bad we lost all the old clues... because this SURE feels like a TRICK.
Actually, we didn't LOSE them. They're just in smoothie form now.
SLURP
BF
Mmm!
And we can always find NEW clues. Like this mysterious ONION!
Huh?
You don't want to mess with that!
ONIONS make you CRY.
Come ON!
ONIONS make you CRY...? I wonder...
HURRY!

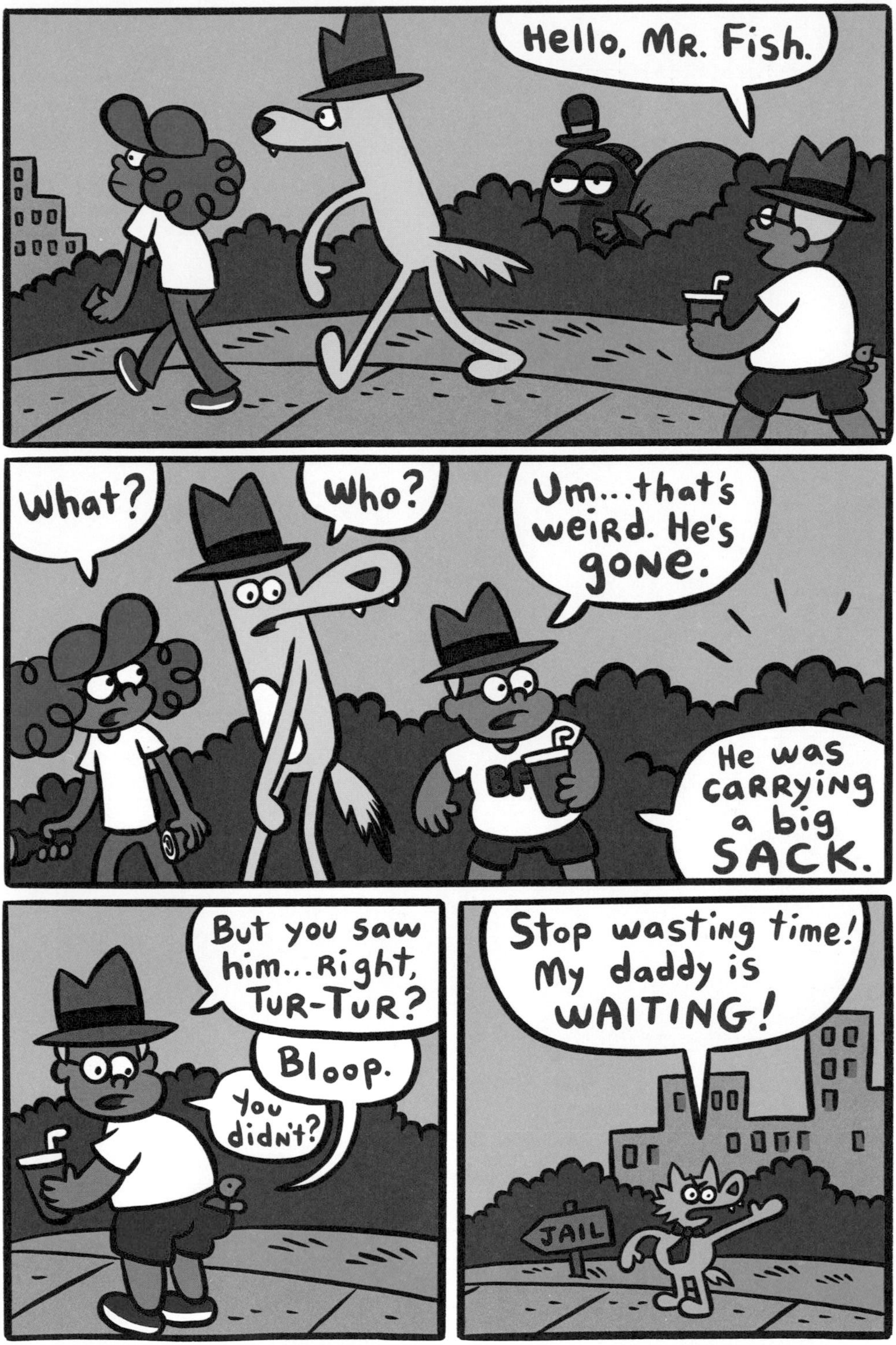
Hello, Mr. Fish.
What?
Who?
Um...that's weird. He's gone.
He was carrying a big SACK.
But you saw him...Right, Tur-Tur?
Bloop.
You didn't?
Stop wasting time! My daddy is WAITING!
JAIL

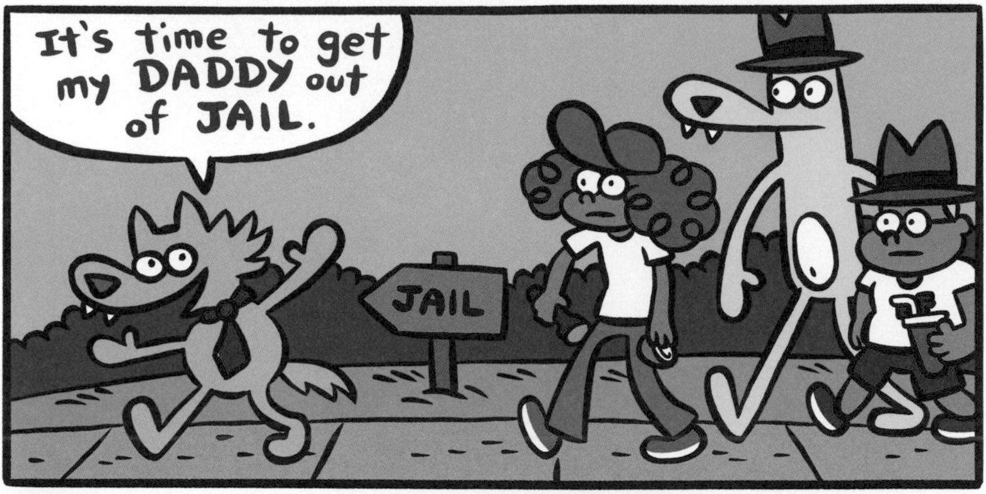
It's time to get my DADDY out of JAIL.
JAIL

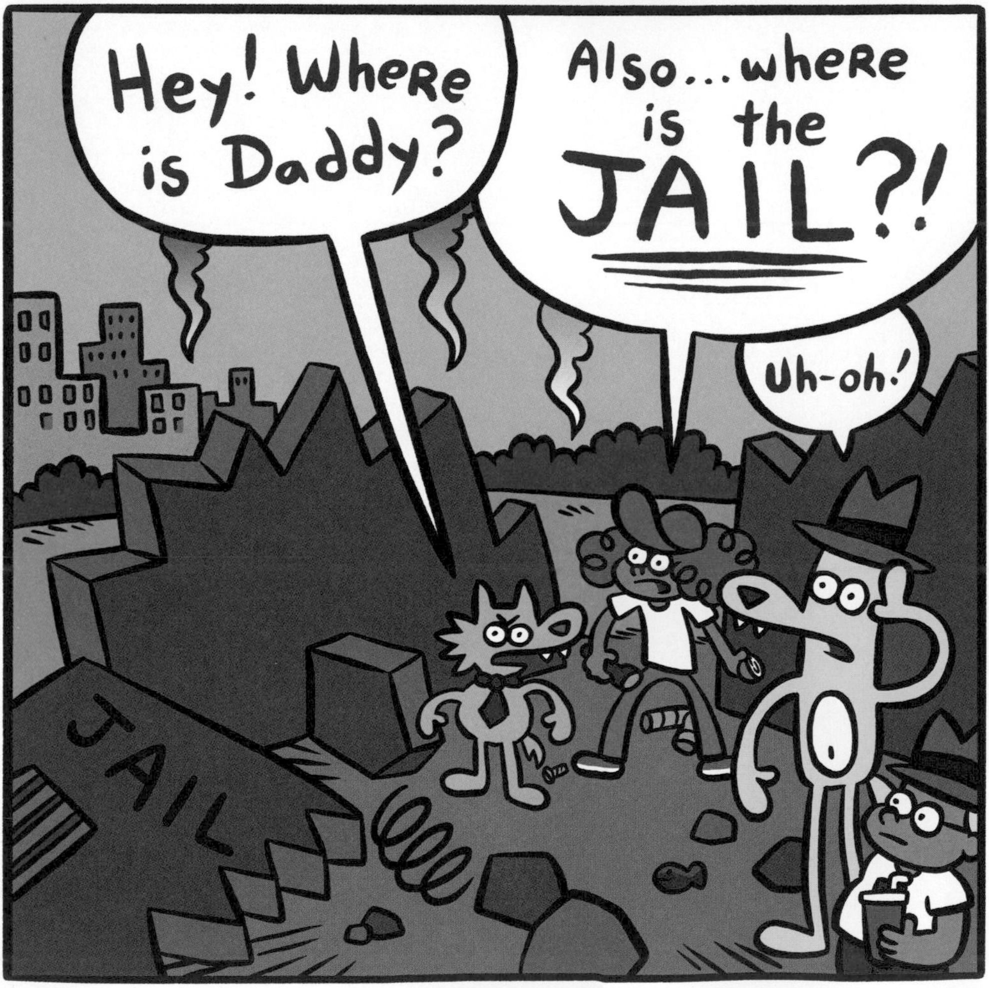
Hey! Where is Daddy?
Also... where is the JAIL?!
Uh-oh!
JAIL

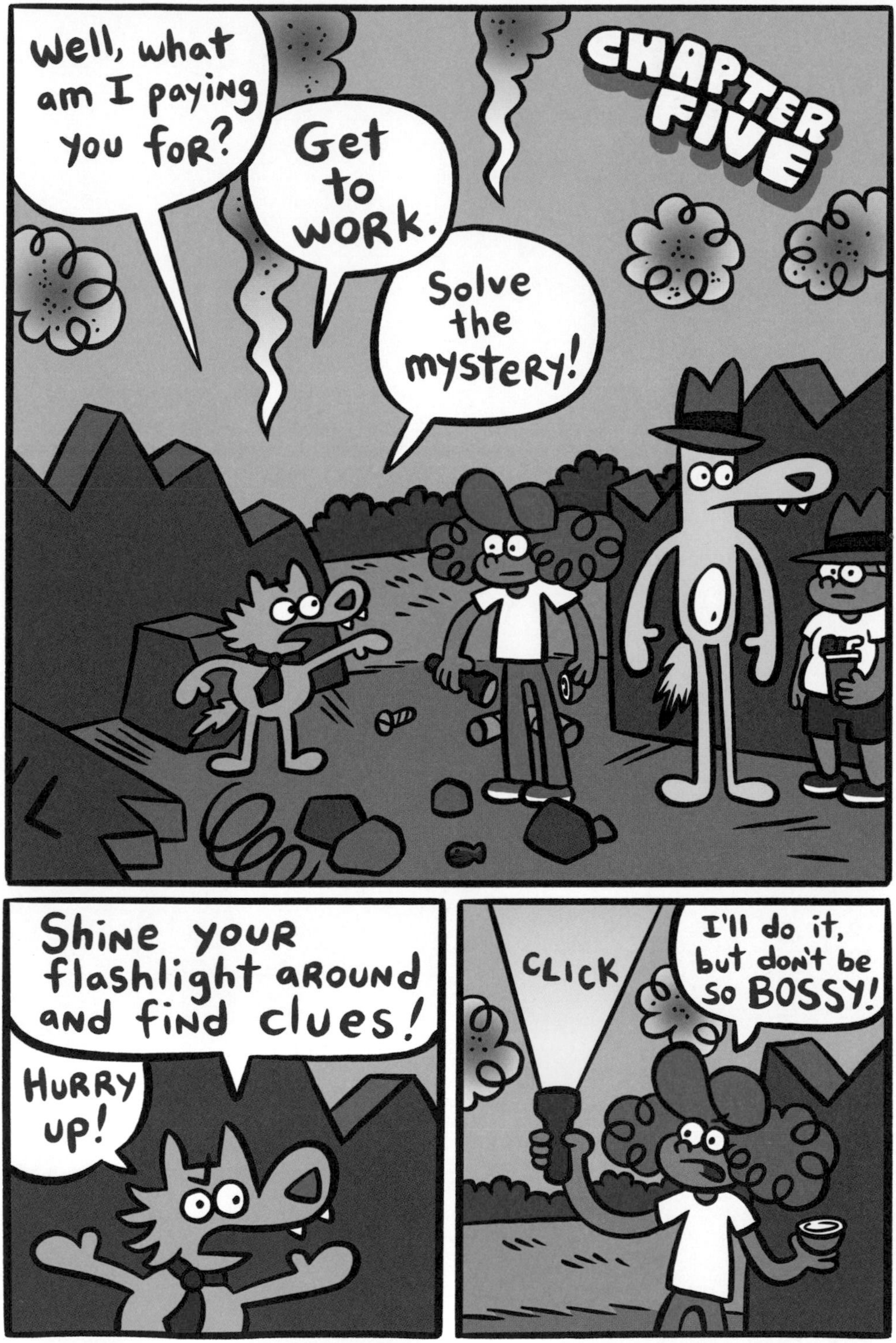
CHAPTER FIVE
Well, what am I paying you for?
Get to WORK.
Solve the mystery!
Shine your flashlight around and find clues!
HURRY up!
CLICK
I'll do it, but don't be so BOSSY!

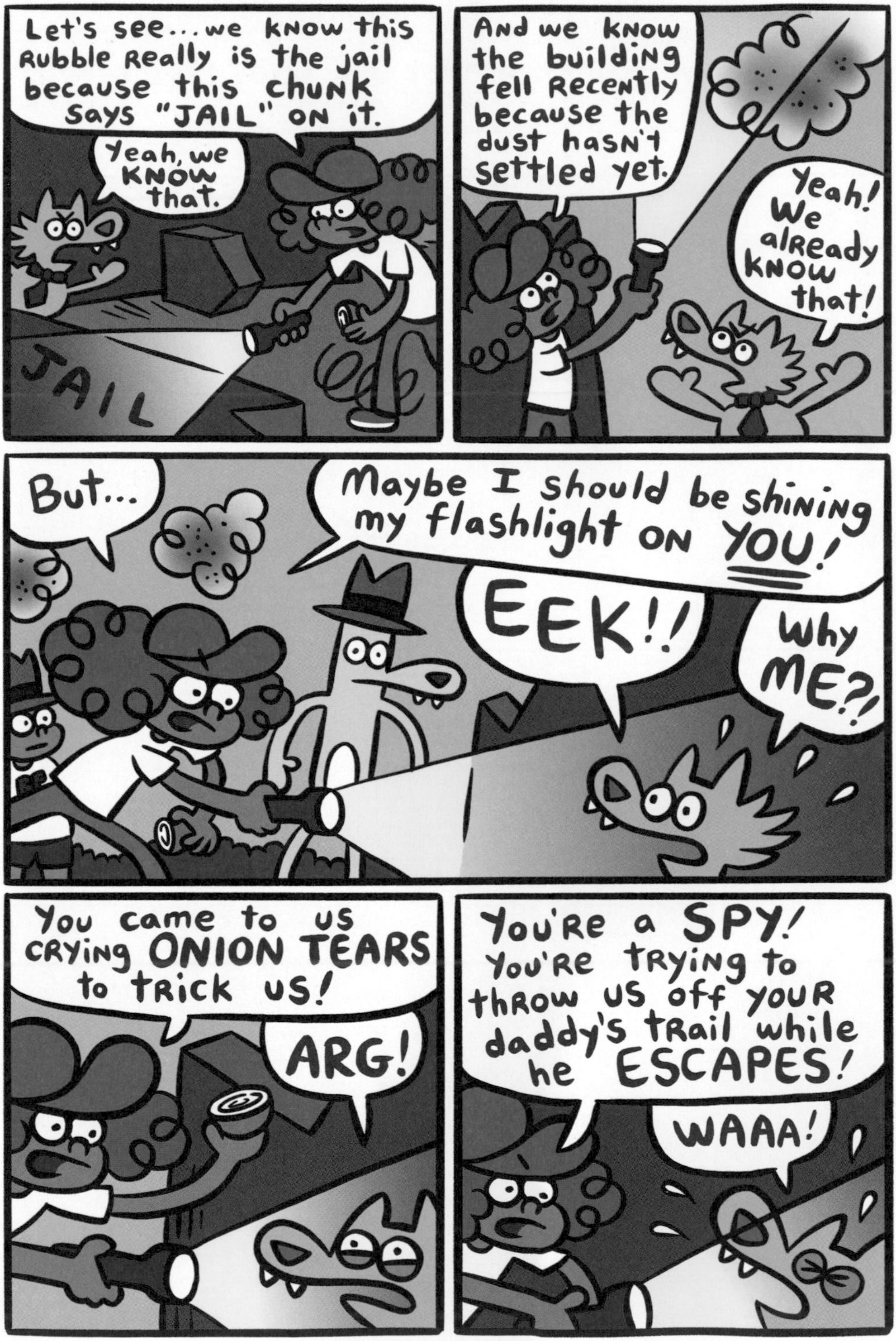
Let's see... we know this Rubble Really is the jail because this chunk says "JAIL" on it.
Yeah, we KNOW that.
JAIL
And we know the building fell Recently because the dust hasn't settled yet.
Yeah! We already KNOW that!
But...
Maybe I should be shining my flashlight on YOU!
EEK!!
Why ME?!
You came to us crying ONION TEARS to trick us!
ARG!
You're a SPY! You're trying to throw us off your daddy's trail while he ESCAPES!
WAAA!

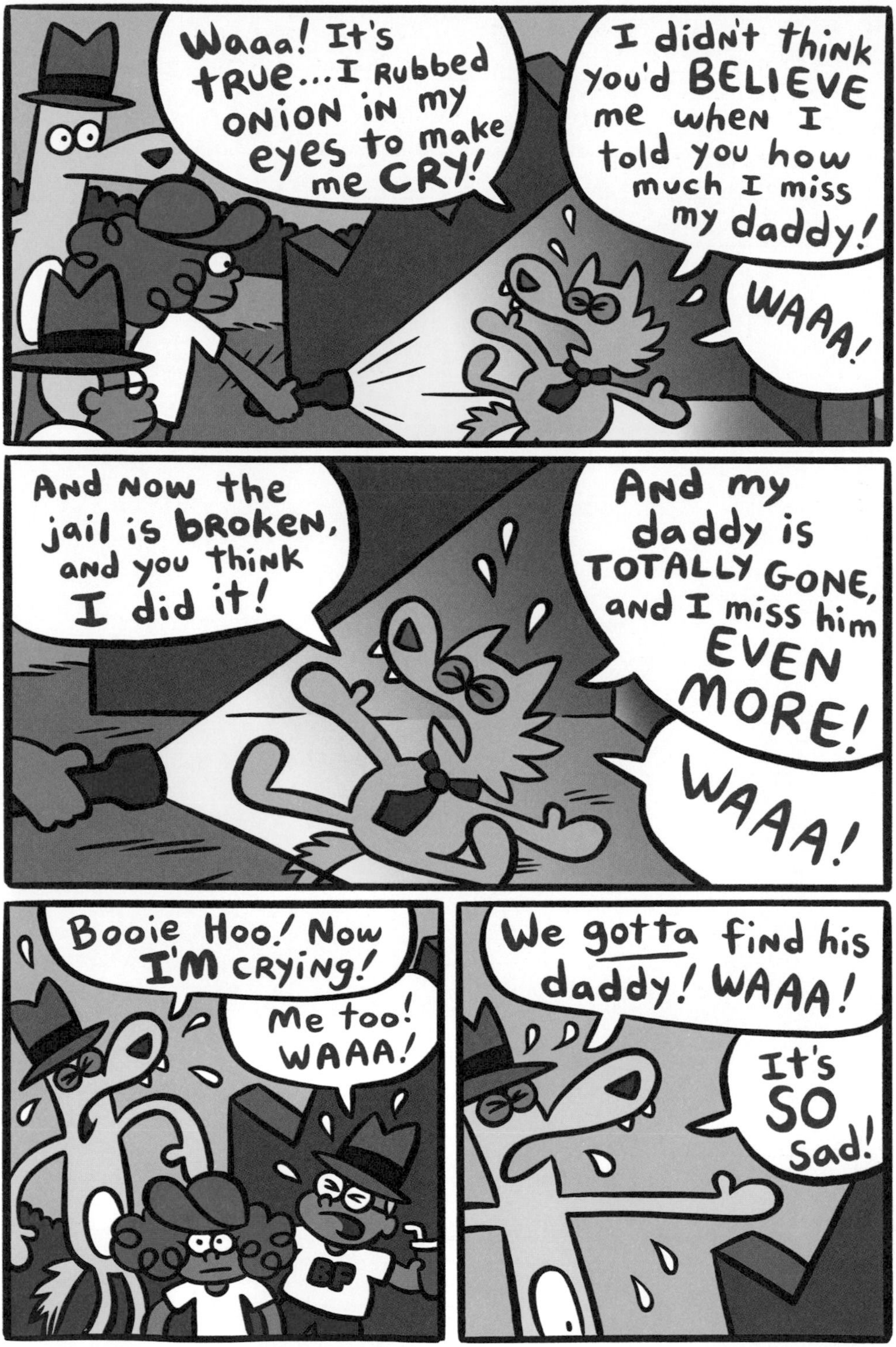
Waaa! It's TRUE...I Rubbed ONION IN my eyes to make me CRY!
I didn't think you'd BELIEVE me when I told you how much I miss my daddy!
WAAA!
And now the jail is broken, and you think I did it!
And my daddy is TOTALLY GONE, and I miss him EVEN MORE!
WAAA!
Booie Hoo! Now I'M CRYING!
Me too! WAAA!
BF
We gotta find his daddy! WAAA!
It's SO sad!

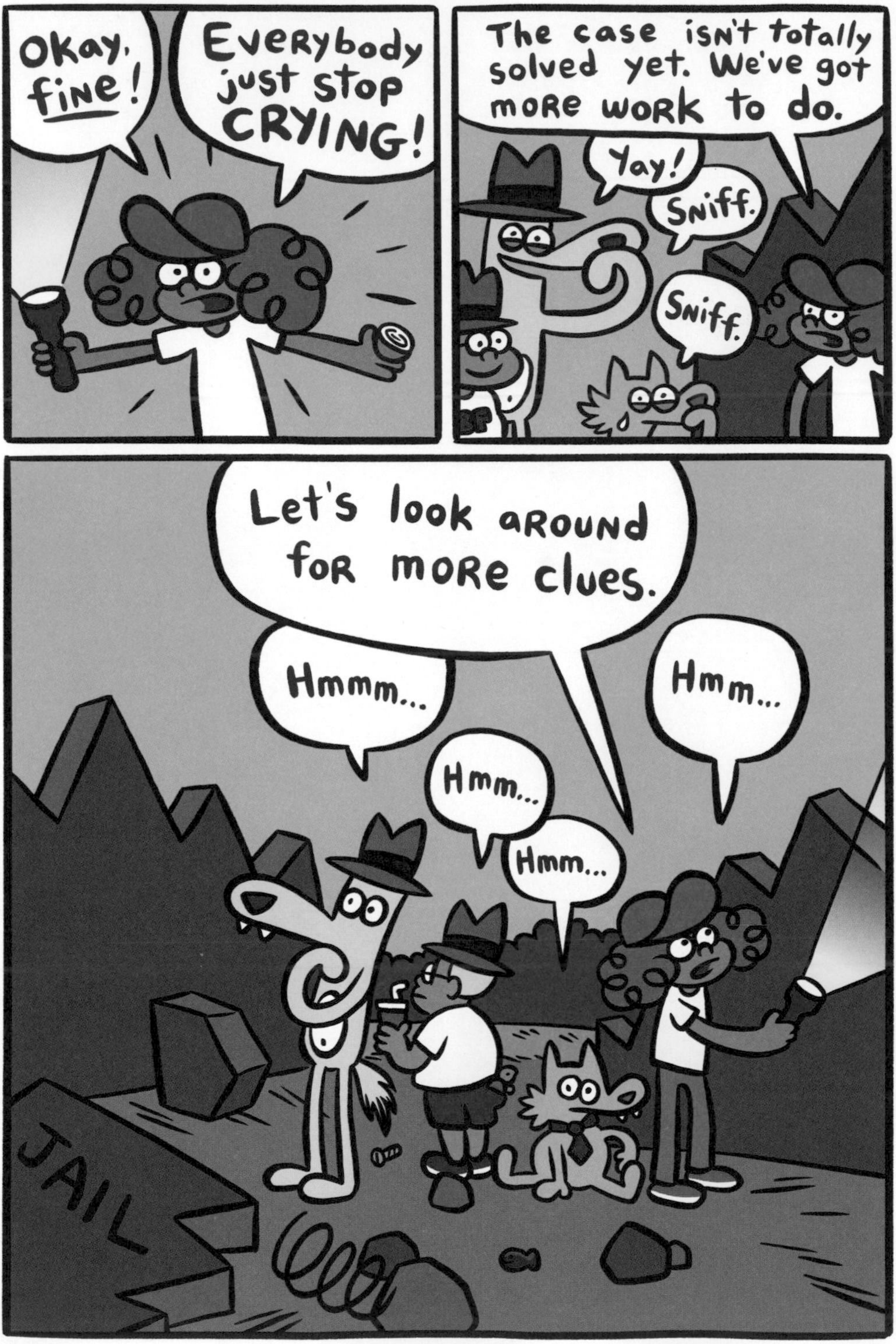
Okay, fine!
Everybody just stop CRYING!
The case isn't totally solved yet. We've got more work to do.
Yay!
Sniff.
Sniff.
BF
Let's look around for more clues.
Hmmm...
Hmm...
Hmm...
Hmm...
JAIL

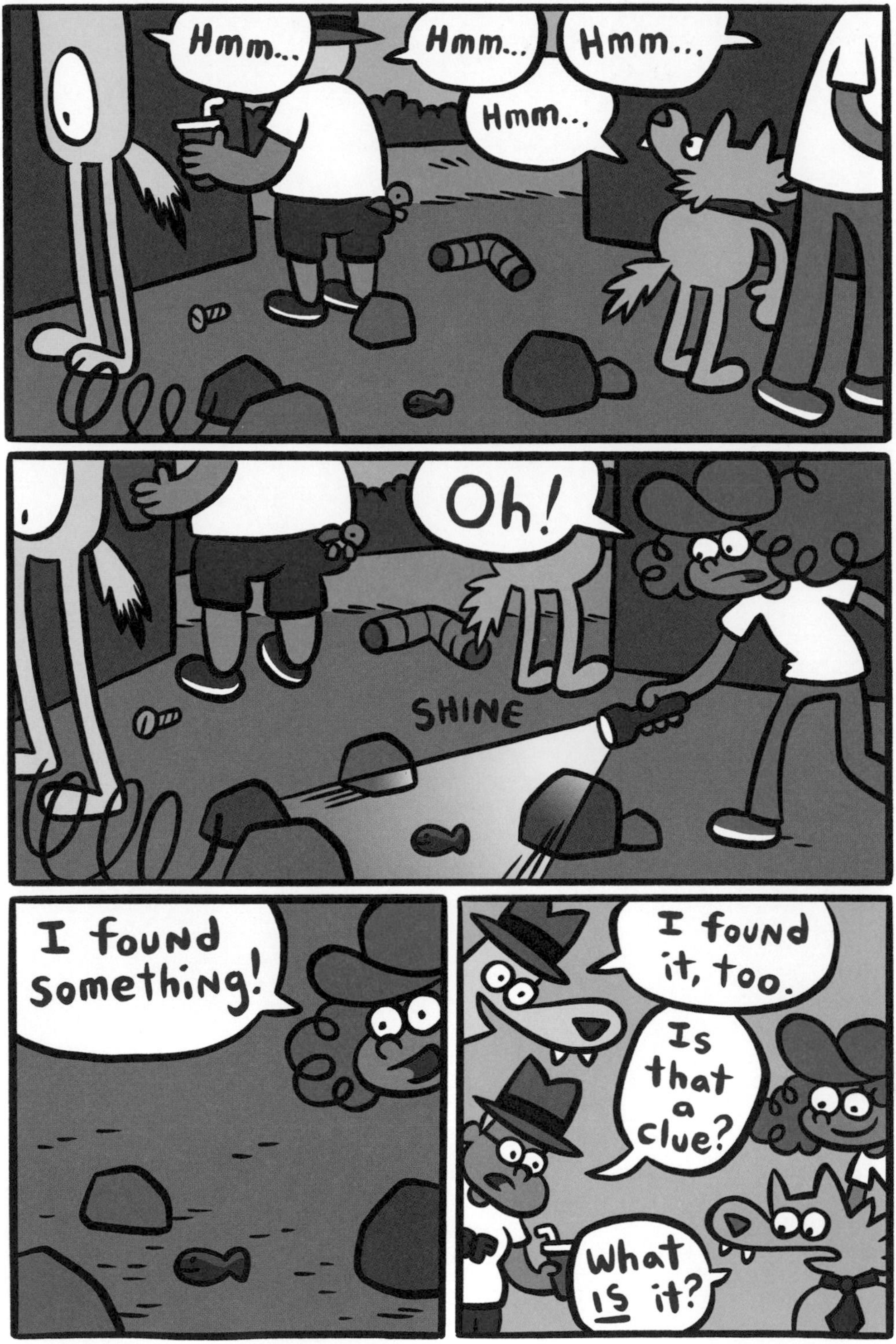
Hmm...
Hmm...
Hmm...
Hmm...
Oh!
SHINE
I found something!
I found it, too.
Is that a clue?
What IS it?

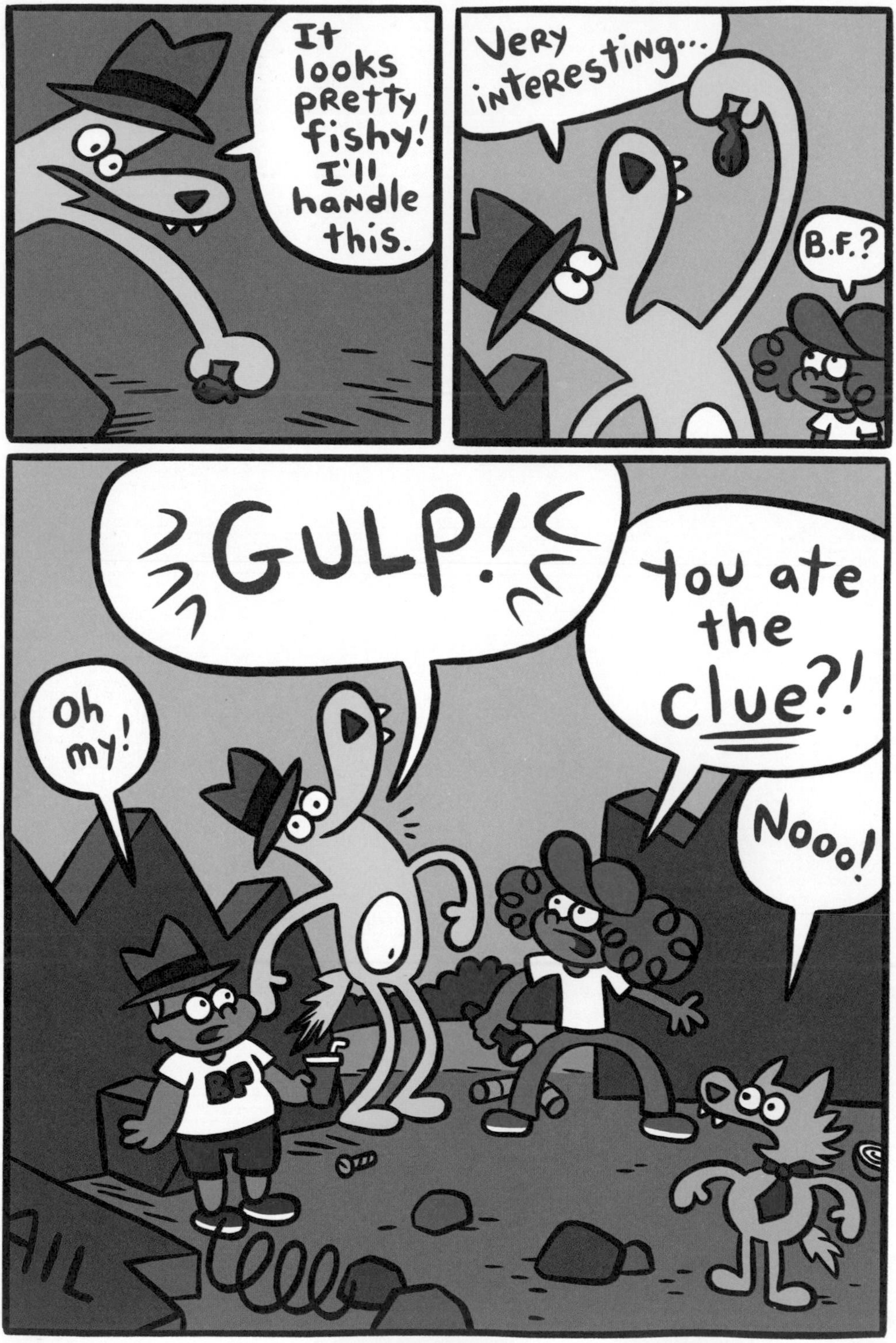
It looks pretty fishy! I'll handle this.
Very interesting...
B.F.?
GULP!
You ate the clue?!
Oh my!
Nooo!

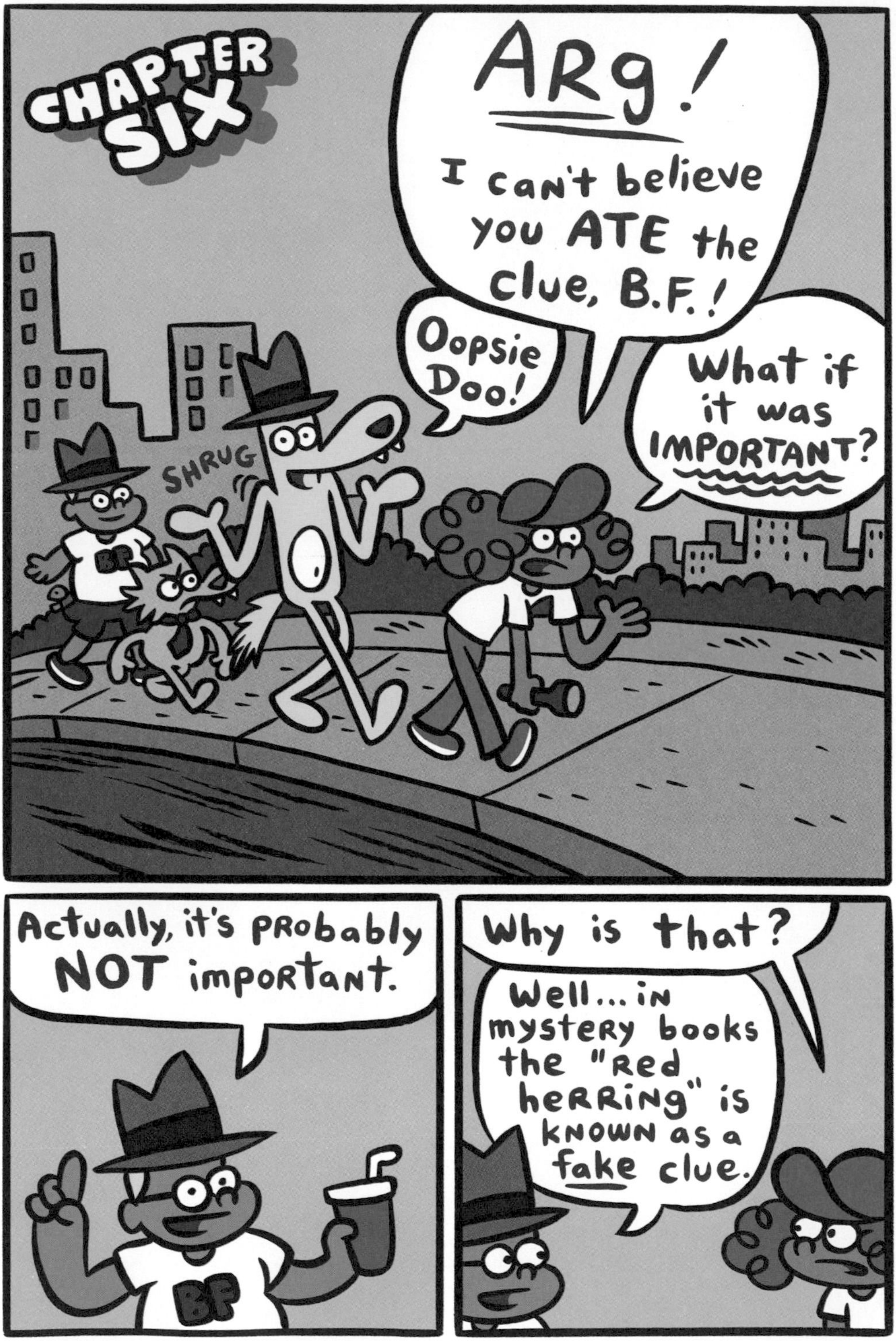
CHAPTER SIX
ARG!
I can't believe you ATE the clue, B.F.!
Oopsie Doo!
SHRUG
What if it was IMPORTANT?
Actually, it's probably NOT important.
Why is that?
Well... in mystery books the "red herring" is known as a fake clue.

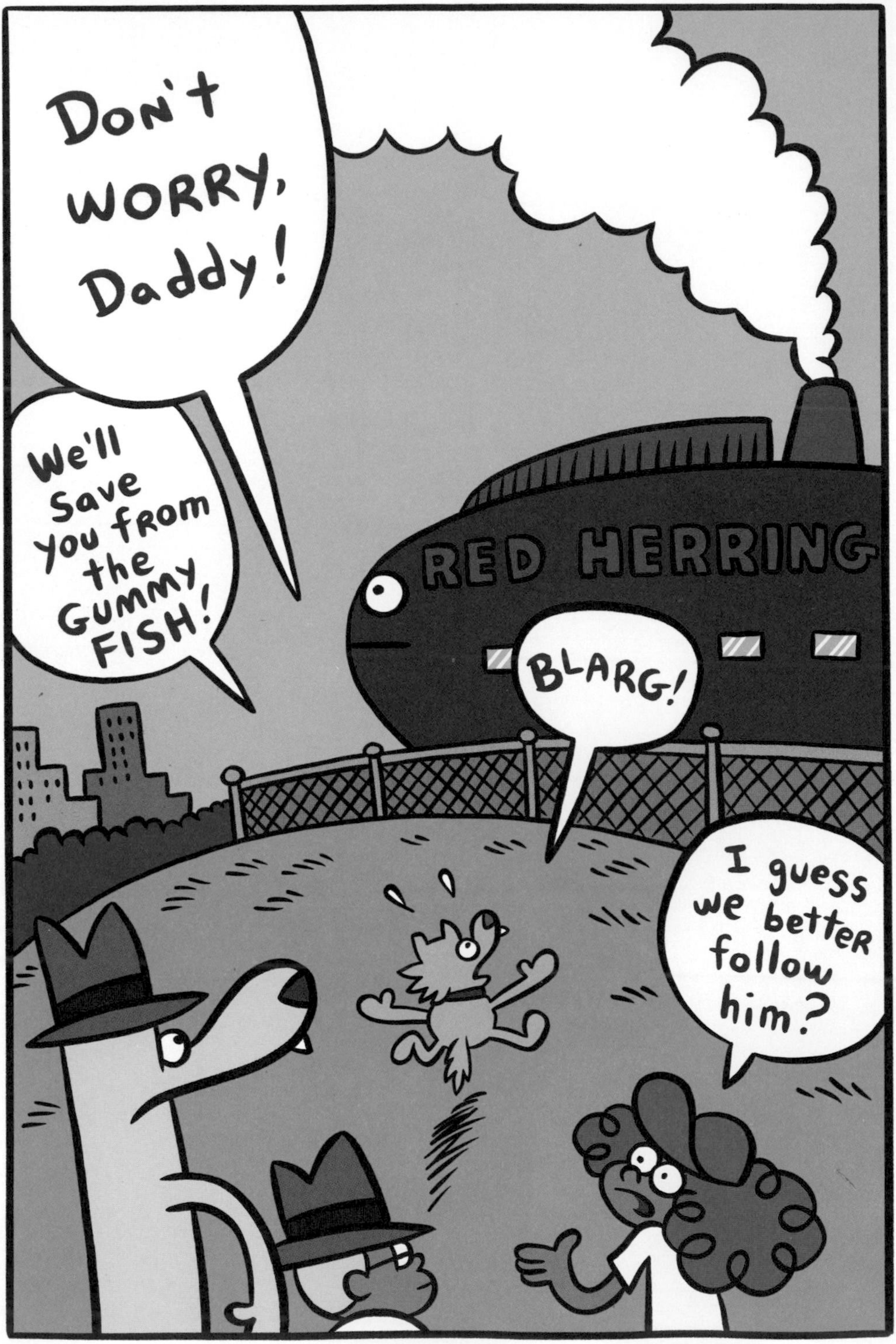
Don't WORRY, Daddy!
We'll save you from the GUMMY FISH!
RED HERRING
BLARG!
I guess we better follow him?

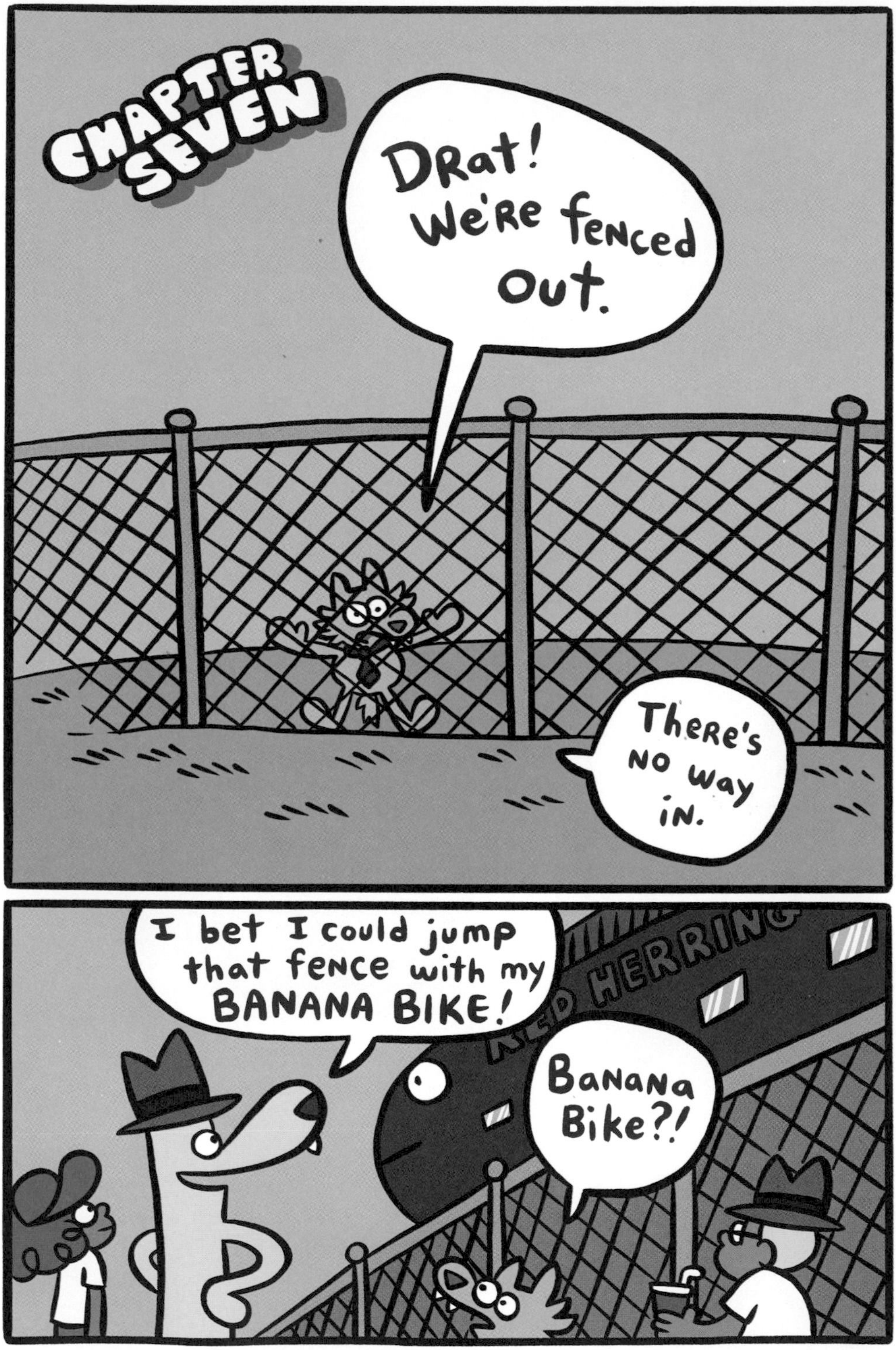
CHAPTER SEVEN
Drat! We're fenced out.
There's no way in.
I bet I could jump that fence with my BANANA BIKE!
RED HERRING
Banana Bike?!

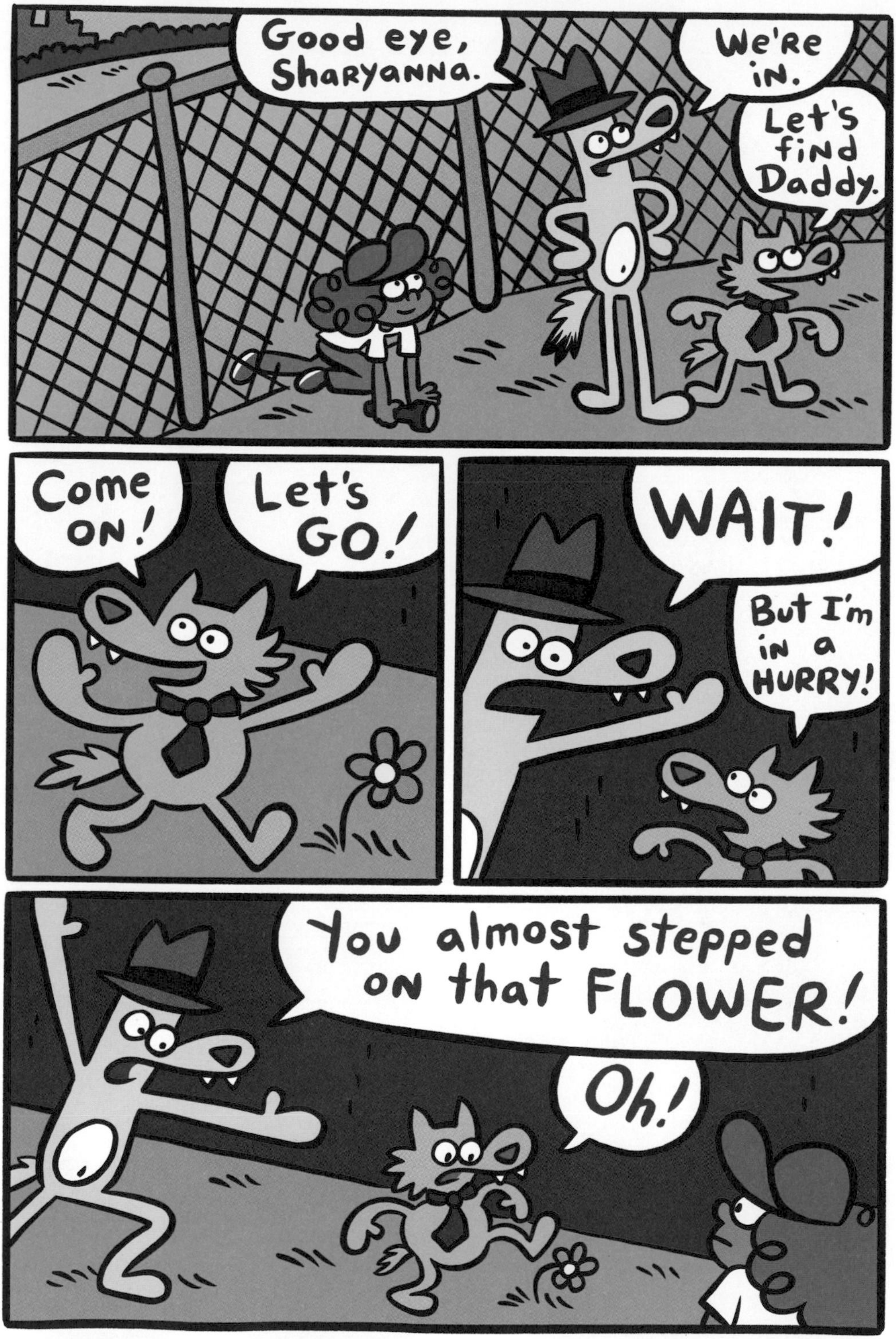
Good eye, Sharyanna.
We're in.
Let's find Daddy.
Come on!
Let's GO!
WAIT!
But I'm in a HURRY!
You almost stepped on that FLOWER!
Oh!

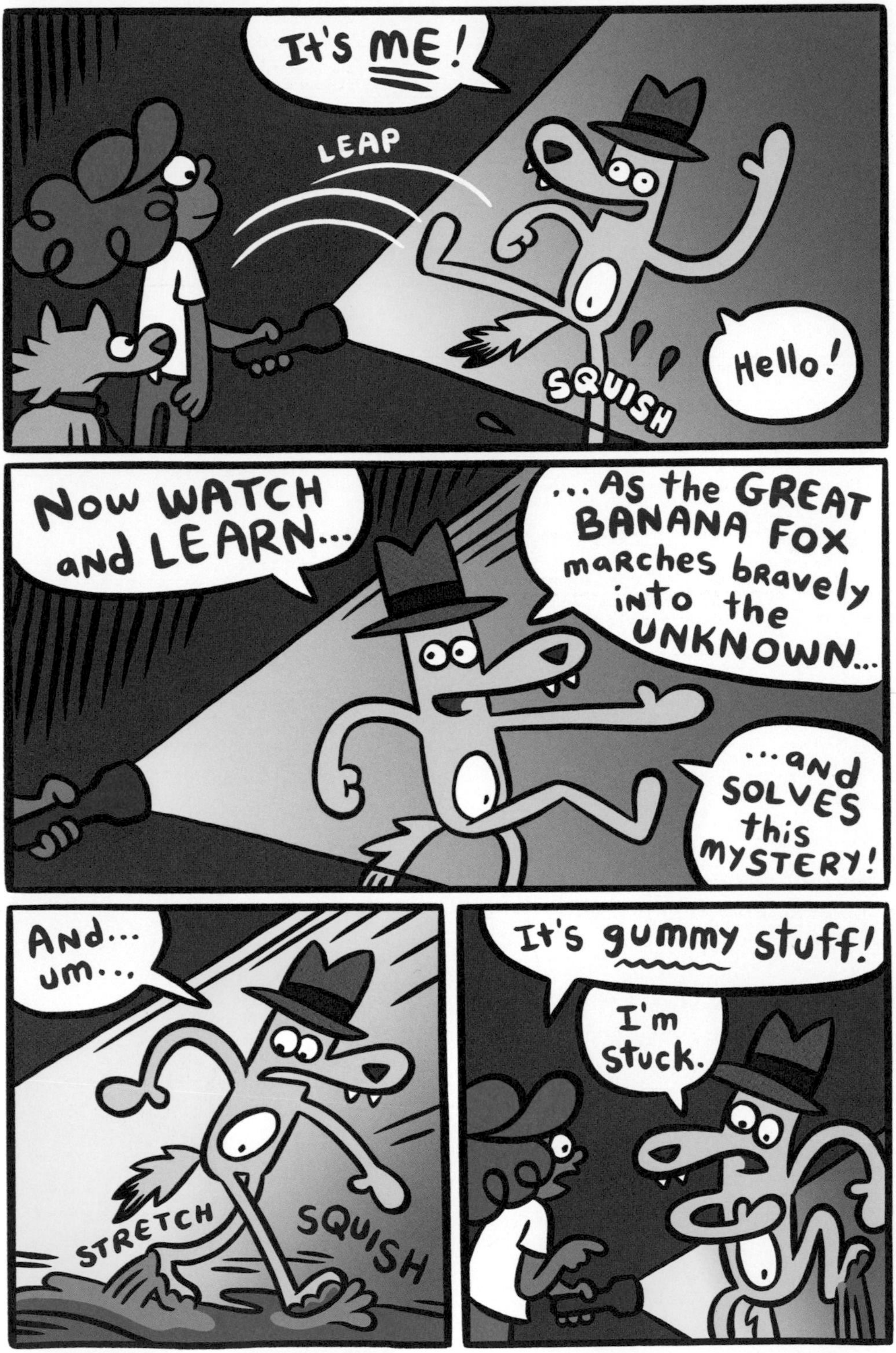
It's ME!
LEAP
SQUISH
Hello!
Now WATCH and LEARN...
...As the GREAT BANANA FOX marches bravely into the UNKNOWN...
...and SOLVES this MYSTERY!
And... um...
STRETCH
SQUISH
It's gummy stuff!
I'm stuck.

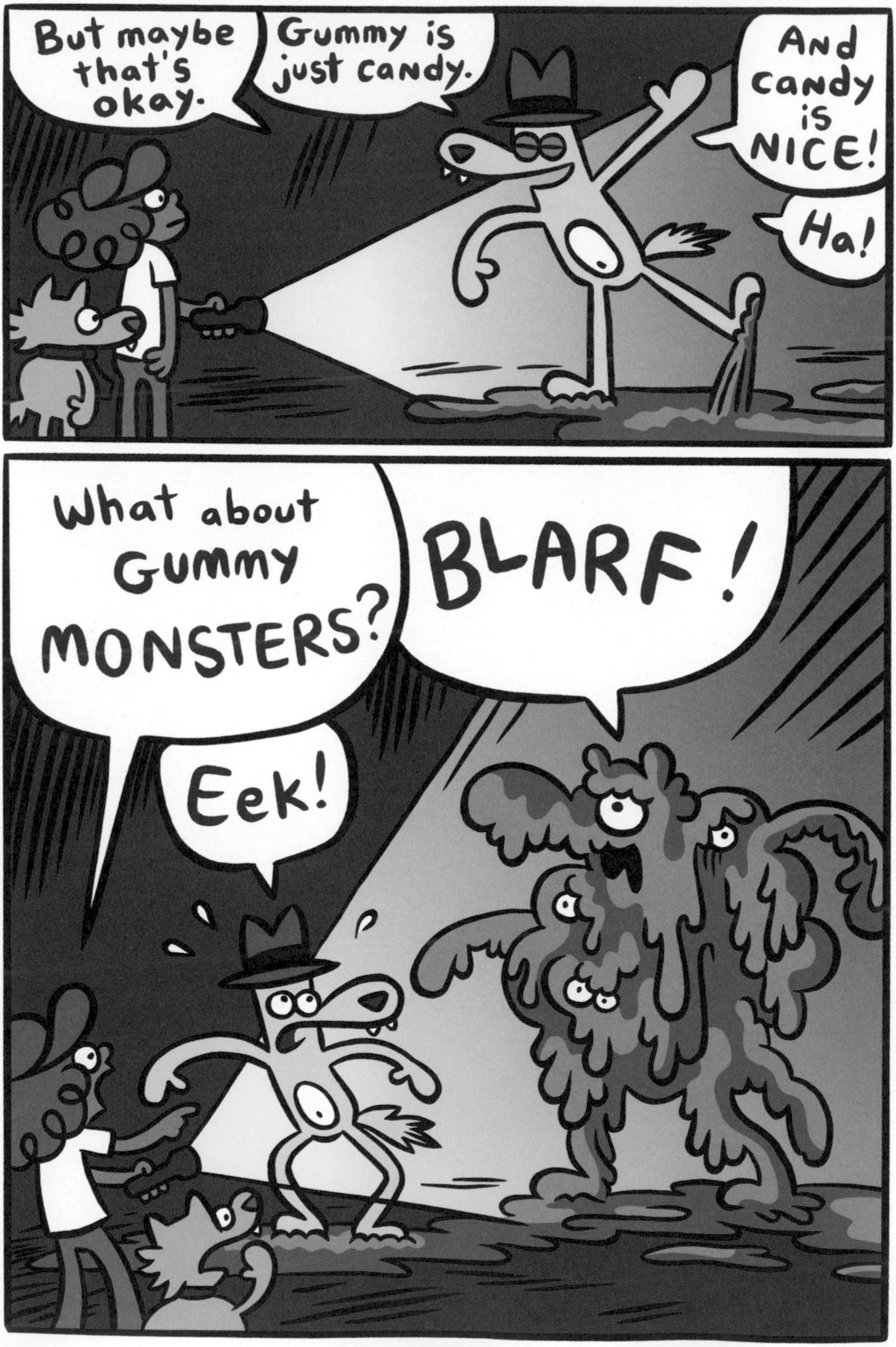
But maybe that's okay.
Gummy is just candy.
And candy is NICE!
Ha!
What about GUMMY MONSTERS?
BLARF!
Eek!

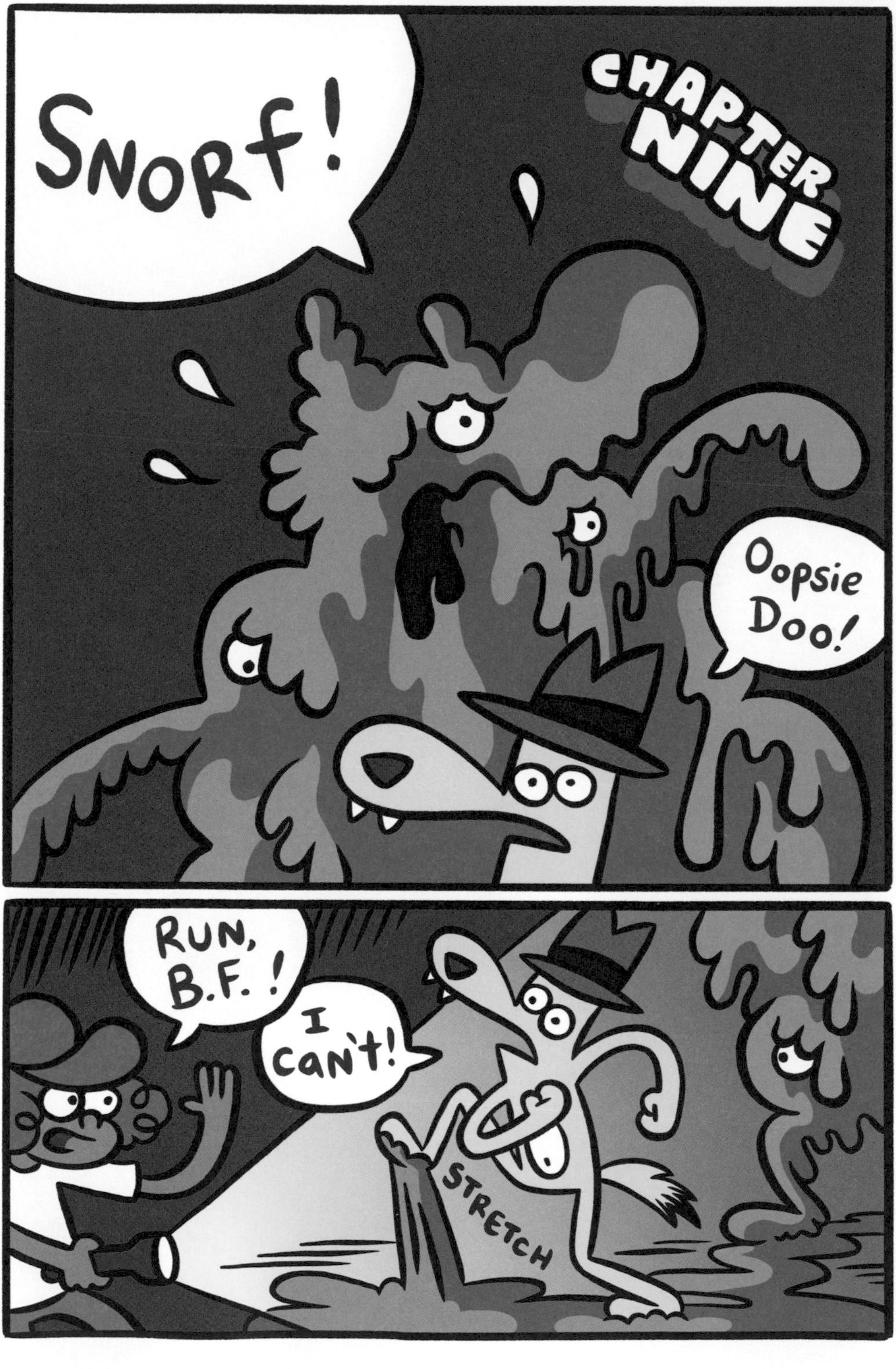
SNORF!
CHAPTER NINE
Oopsie Doo!
RUN, B.F.!
I can't!
STRETCH

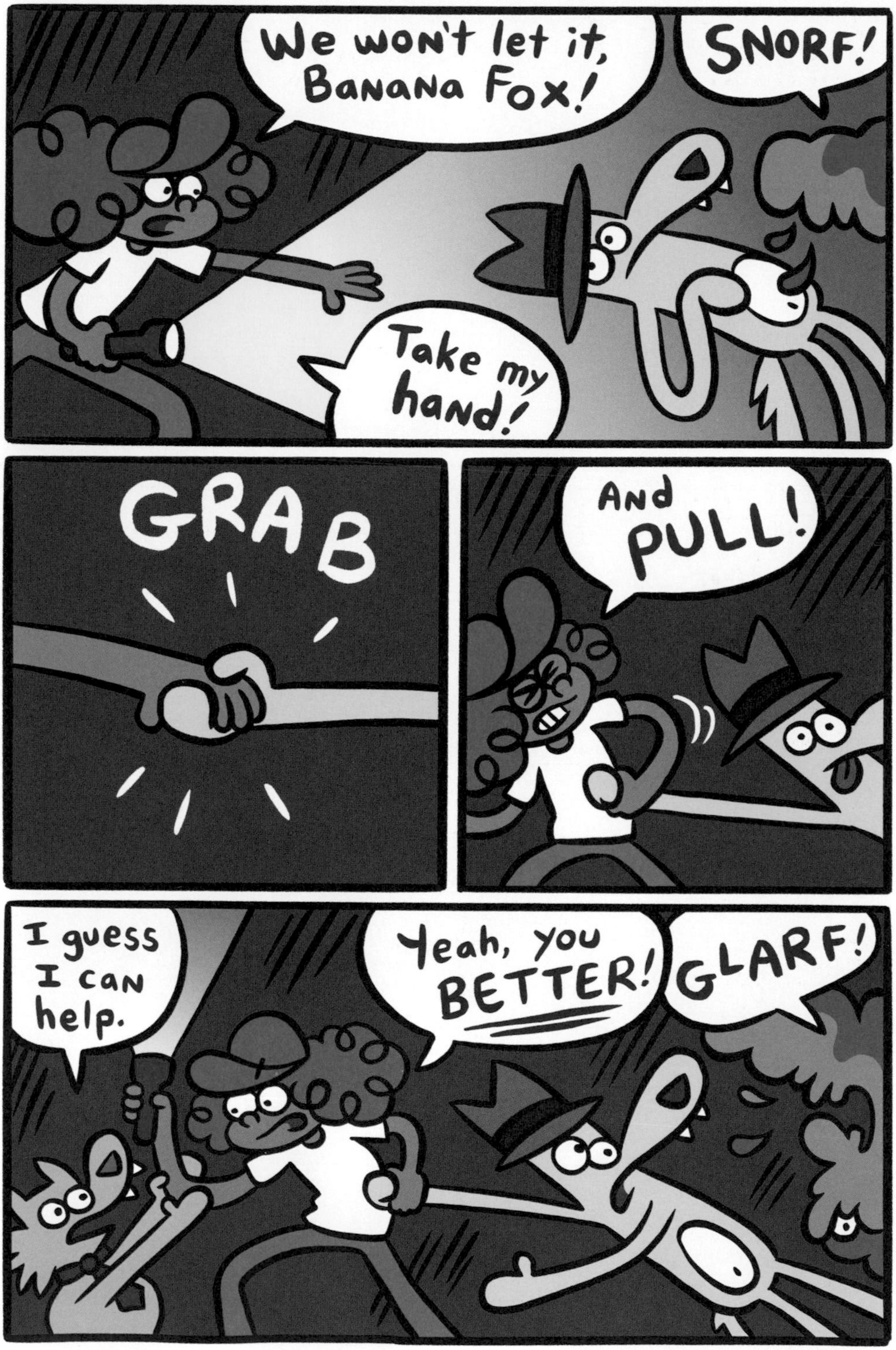
We won't let it, Banana Fox!
SNORF!
Take my hand!
GRAB
AND PULL!
I guess I can help.
Yeah, you BETTER!
GLARF!

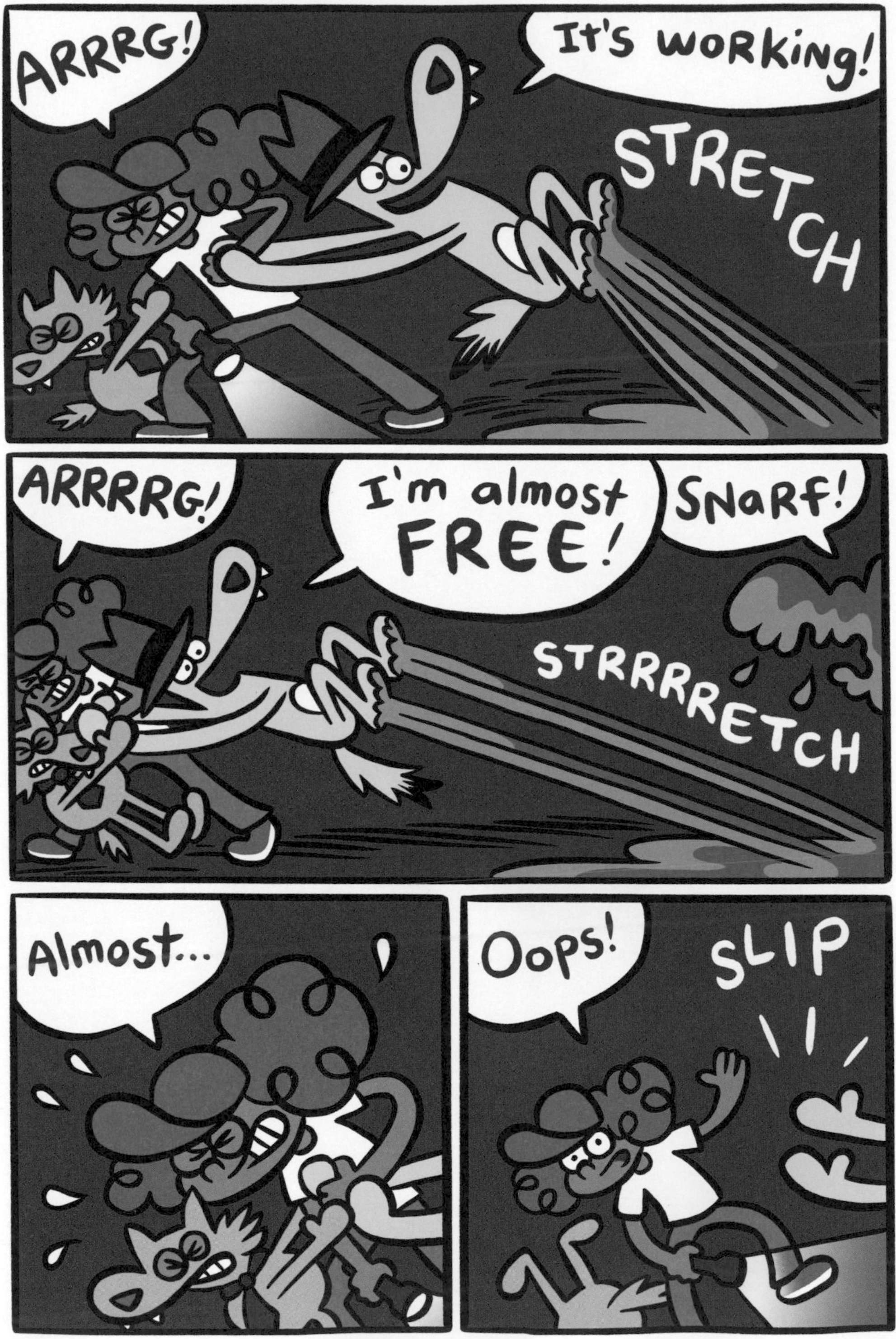
ARRRG!
It's working!
STRETCH
ARRRRG!
I'm almost FREE!
SNARF!
STRRRRRETCH
Almost...
Oops!
SLIP

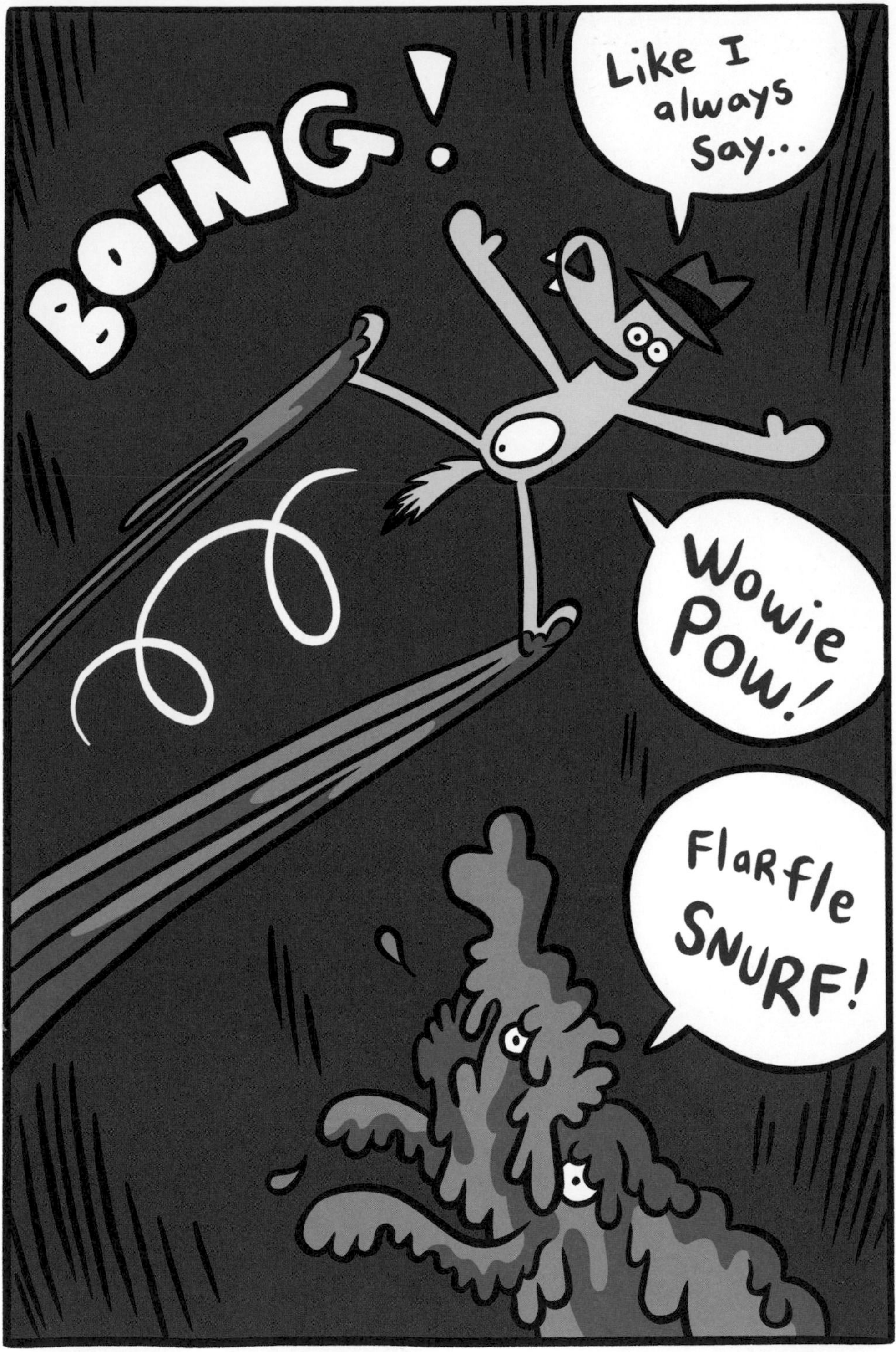
BOING!
Like I always say...
Wowie Pow!
Flarfle SNURF!

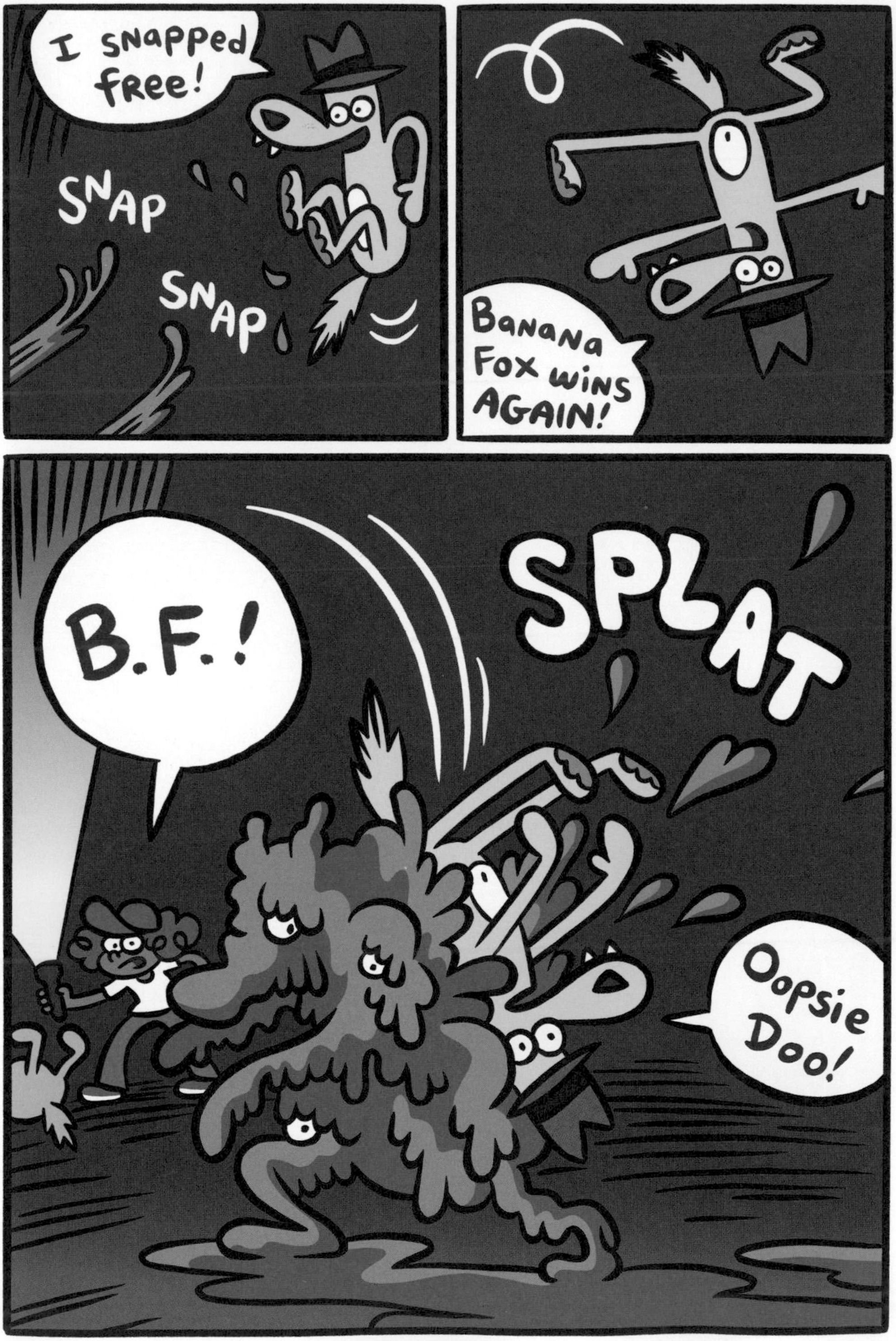
I snapped free!
SNAP
SNAP
Banana Fox wins AGAIN!
B.F.!
SPLAT
Oopsie Doo!

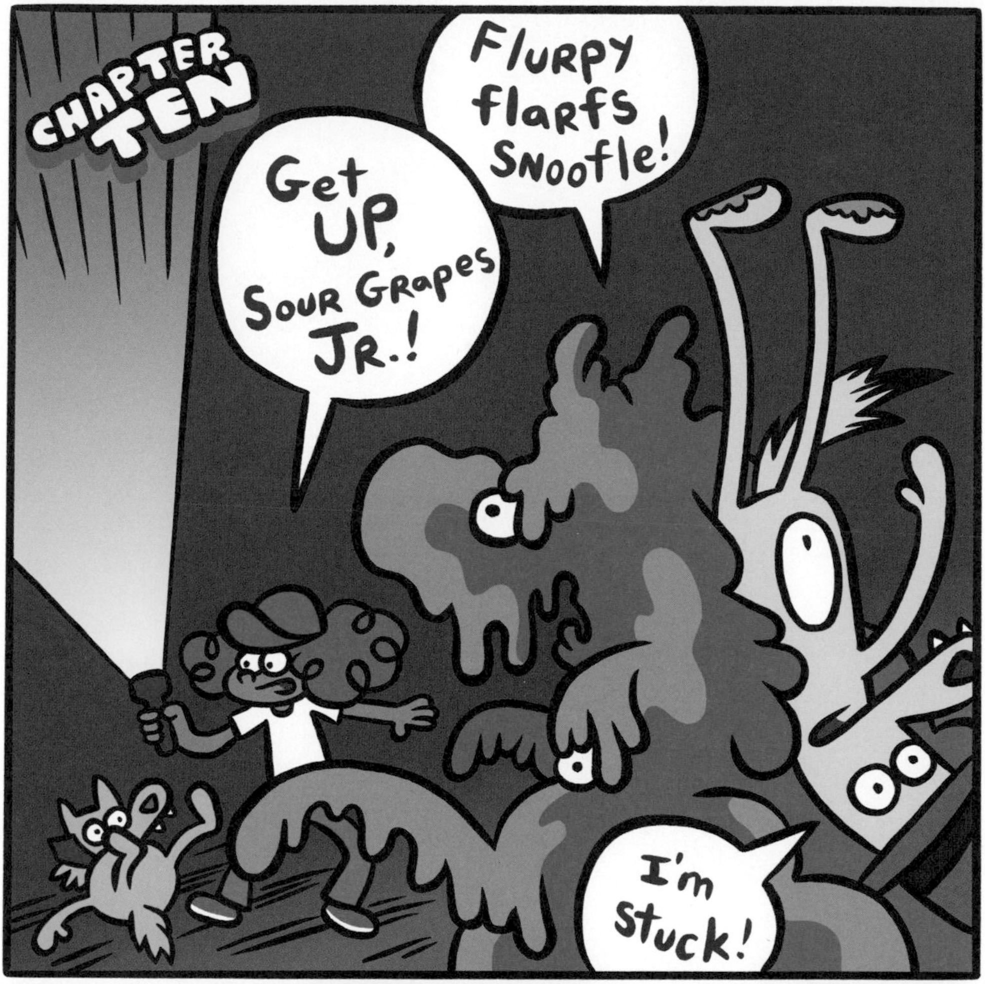
CHAPTER TEN
Flurpy flarfs Snoofle!
Get UP, Sour Grapes Jr.!
I'm stuck!

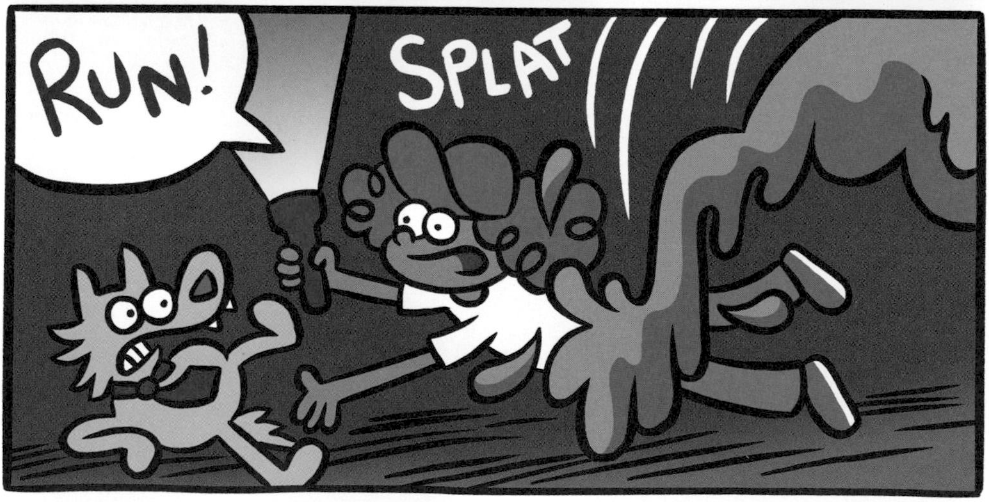
RUN!
SPLAT

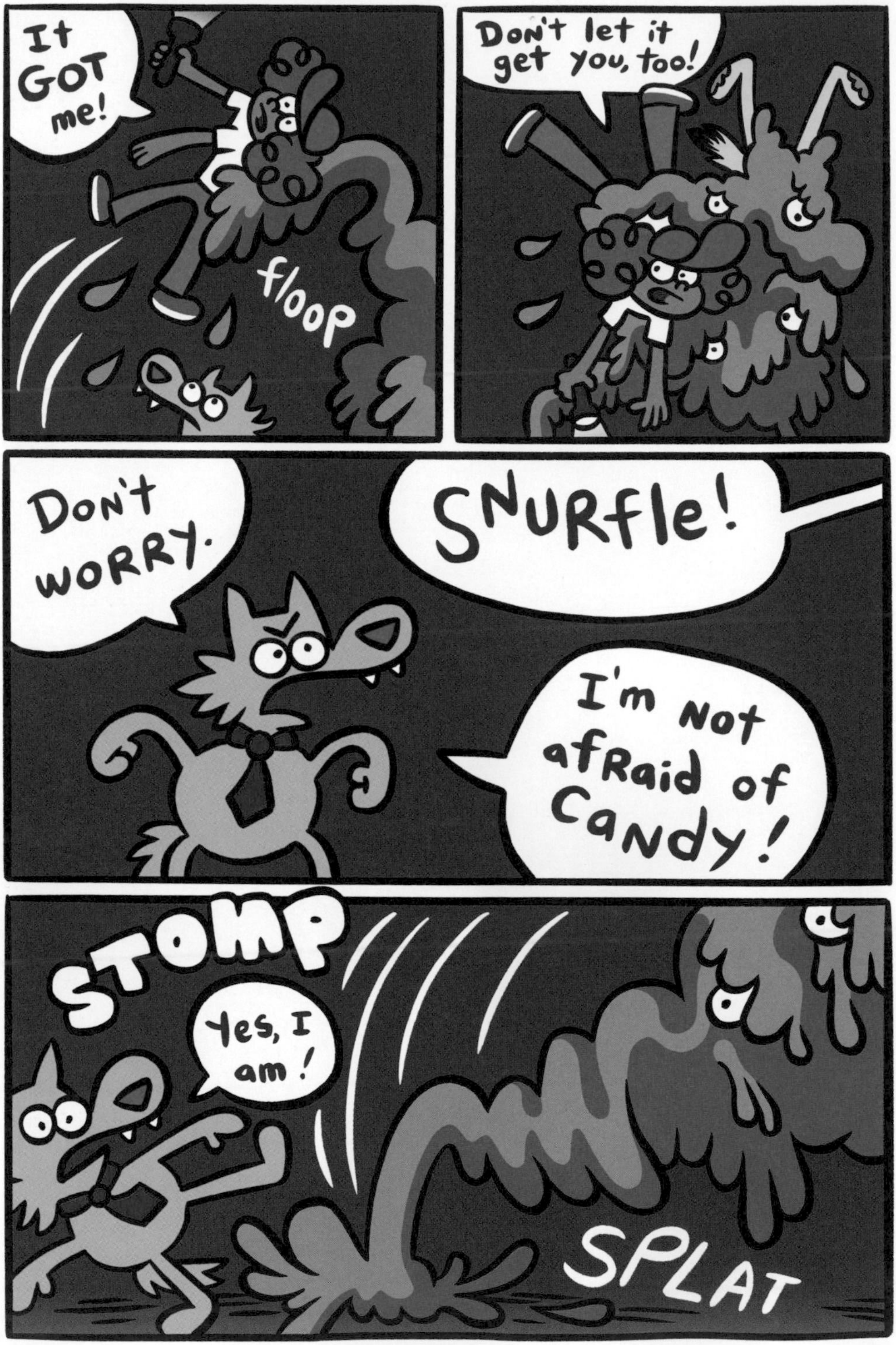
It GOT me!
floop
Don't let it get you, too!
Don't WORRY.
SNURFLE!
I'm NOT afraid of CANDY!
STOMP
Yes, I am!
SPLAT

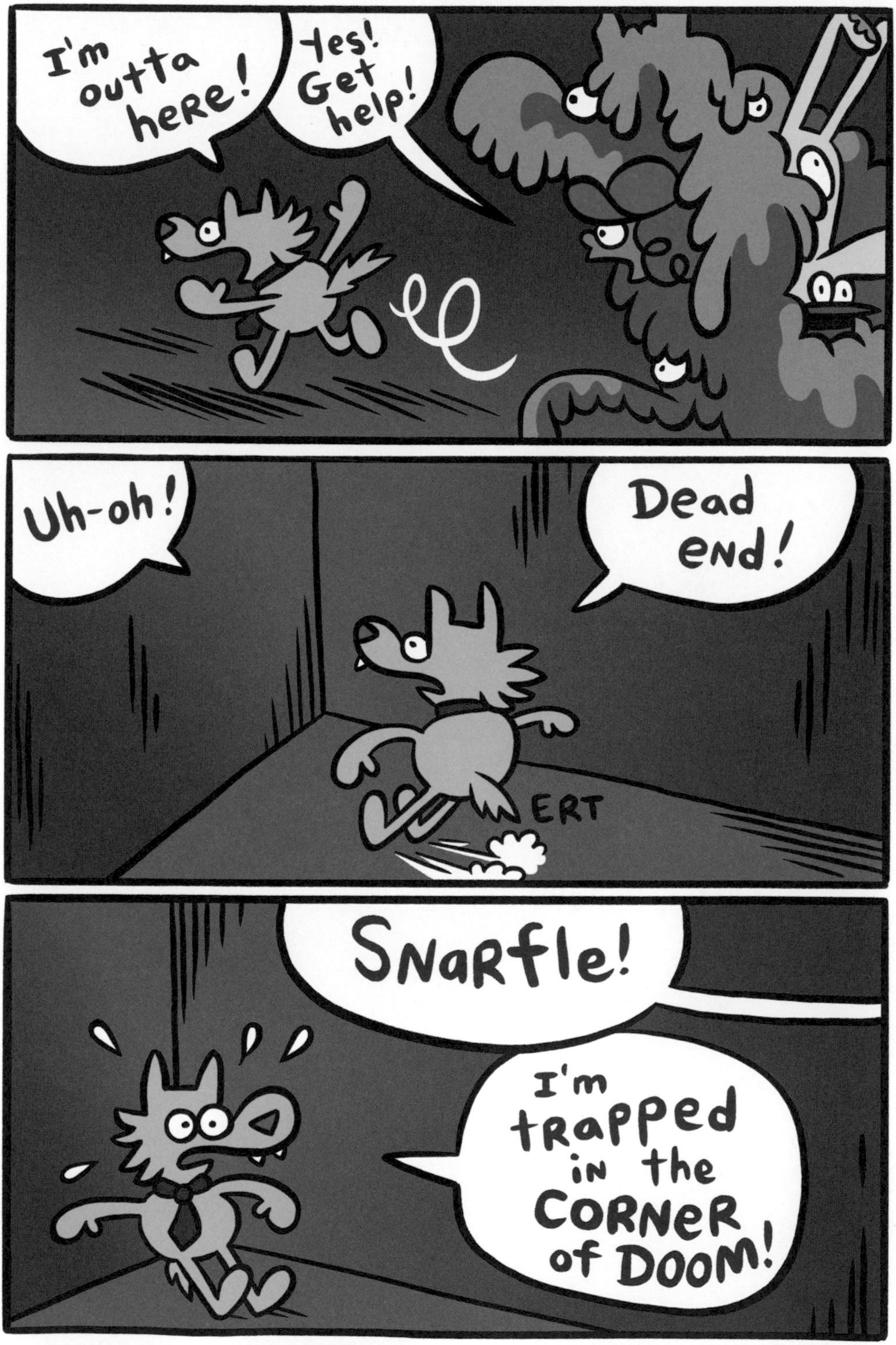
I'm outta here!
Yes! Get help!
Uh-oh!
Dead end!
ERT
Snarfle!
I'm trapped in the CORNER of DOOM!

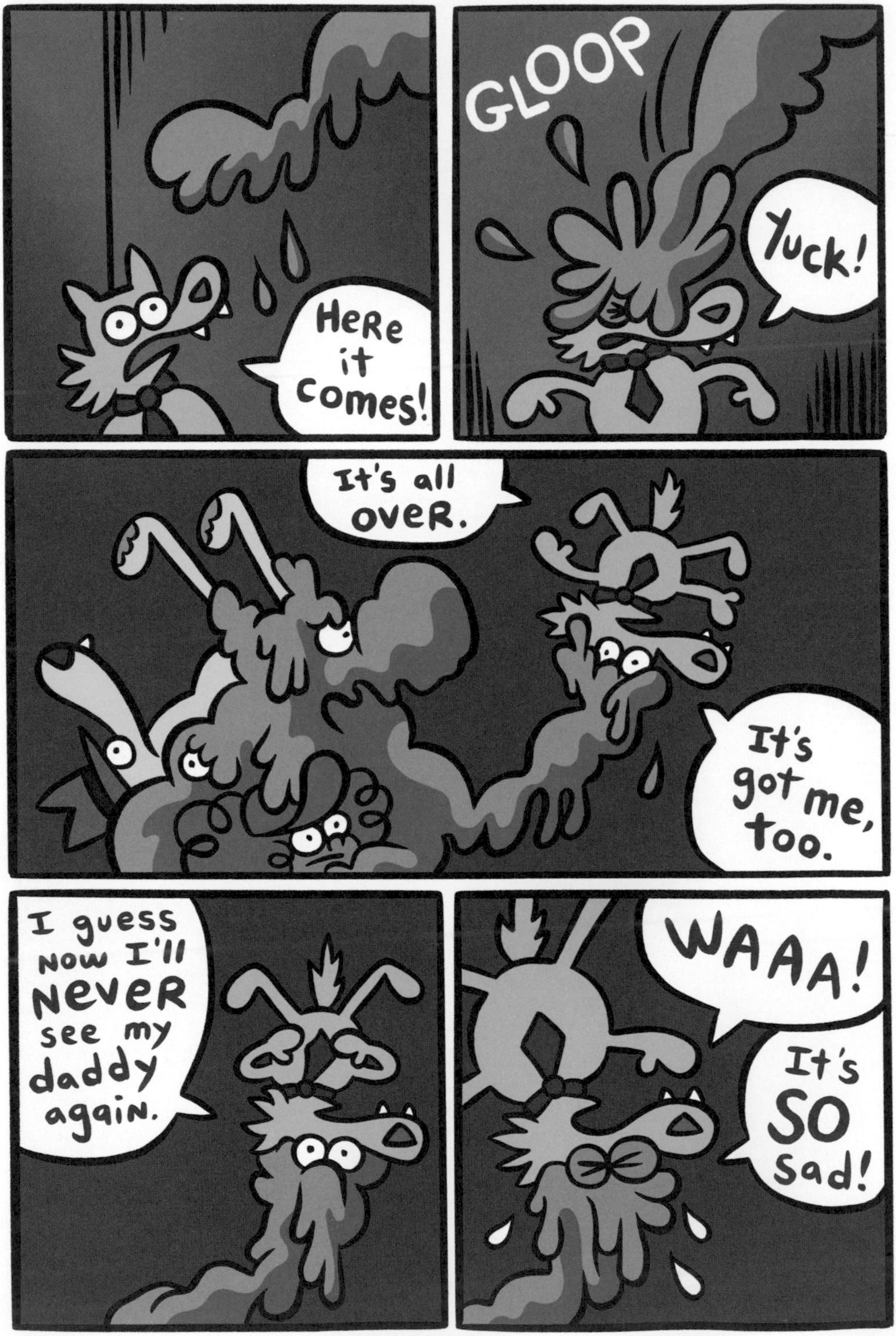
Here it comes!
GLOOP
Yuck!
It's all OVER.
It's got me, too.
I guess now I'll NEVER see my daddy again.
WAAA!
It's SO sad!

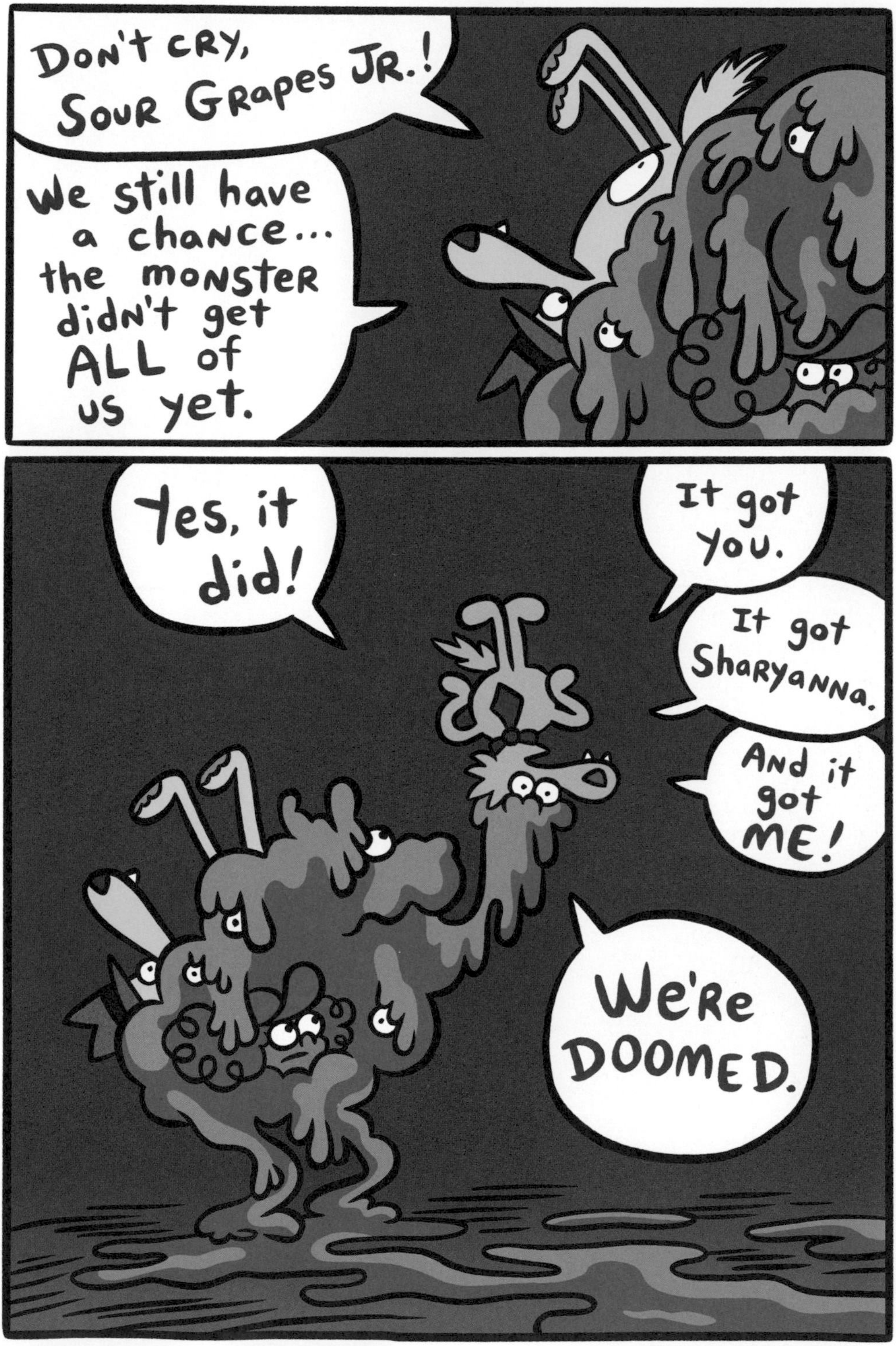
Don't cry, Sour Grapes Jr.!
We still have a chance... the monster didn't get ALL of us yet.
Yes, it did!
It got you.
It got Sharyanna.
And it got ME!
We're DOOMED.

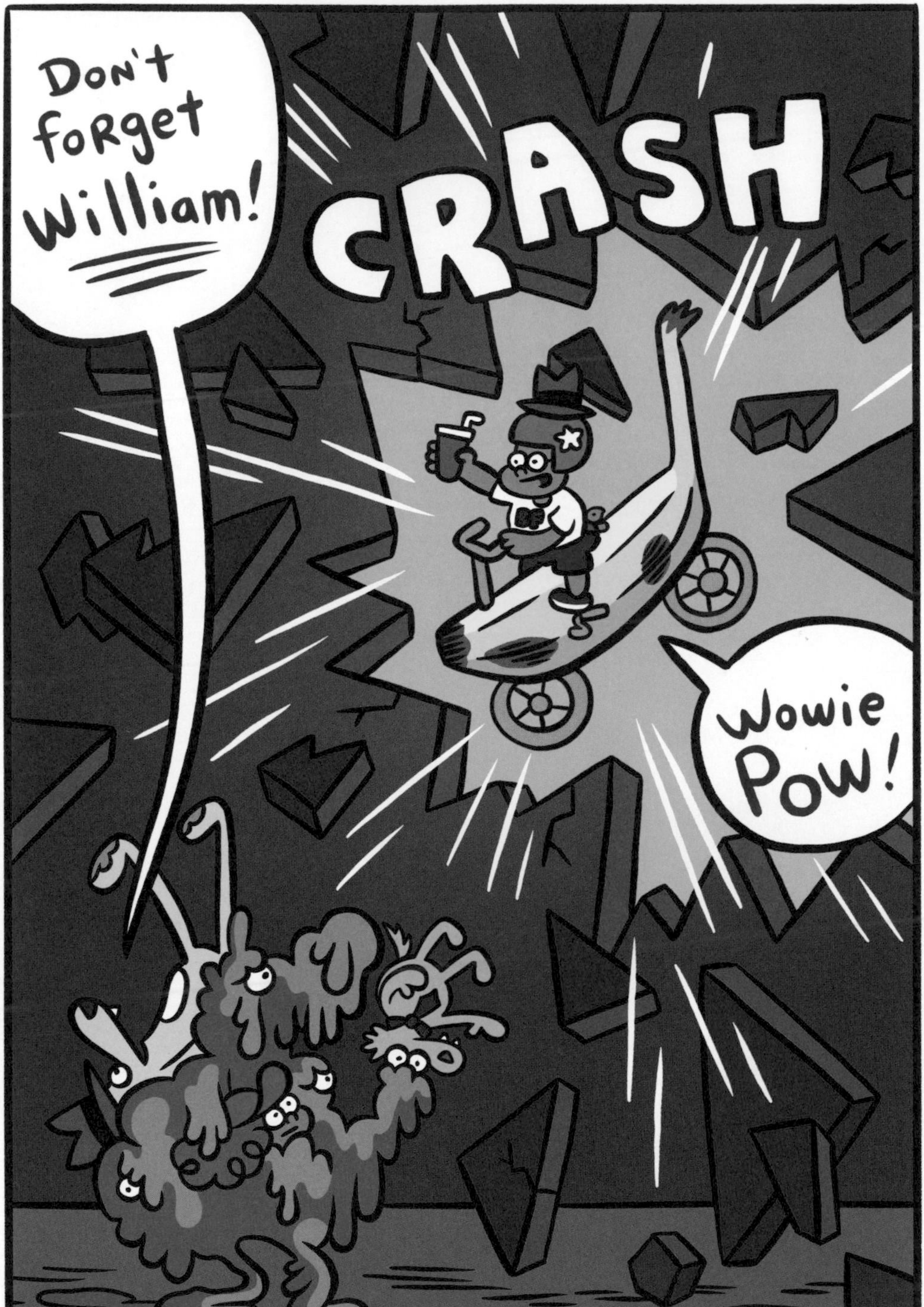
Don't forget William!
CRASH
Wowie Pow!

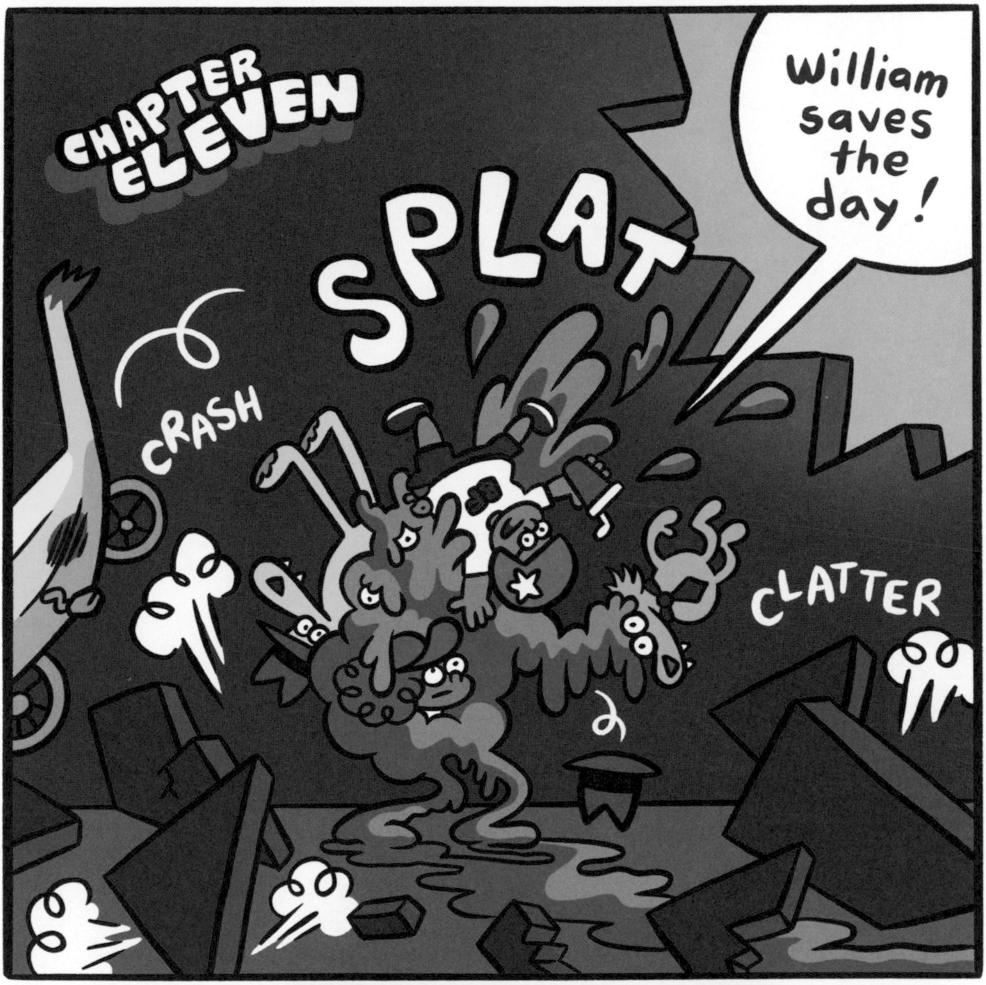
CHAPTER ELEVEN
SPLAT
William saves the day!
CRASH
CLATTER

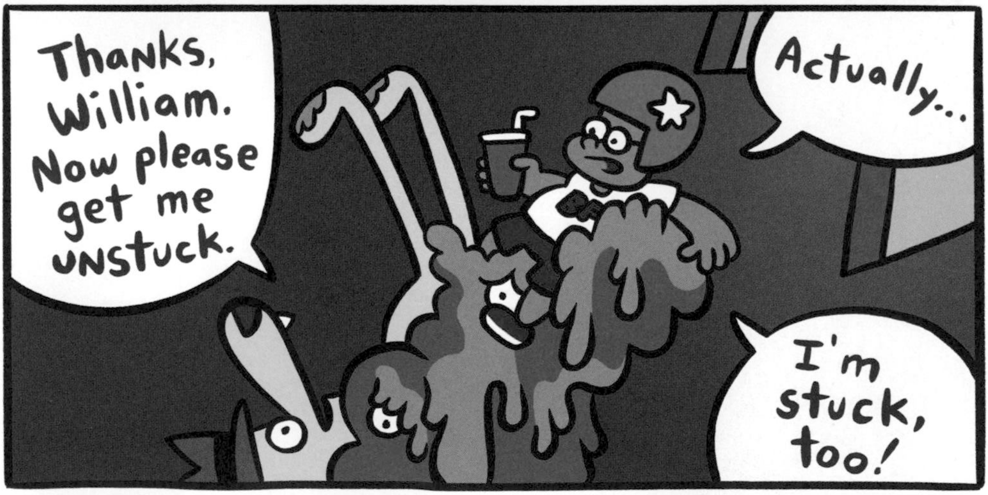
Thanks, William. Now please get me unstuck.
Actually...
I'm stuck, too!

55

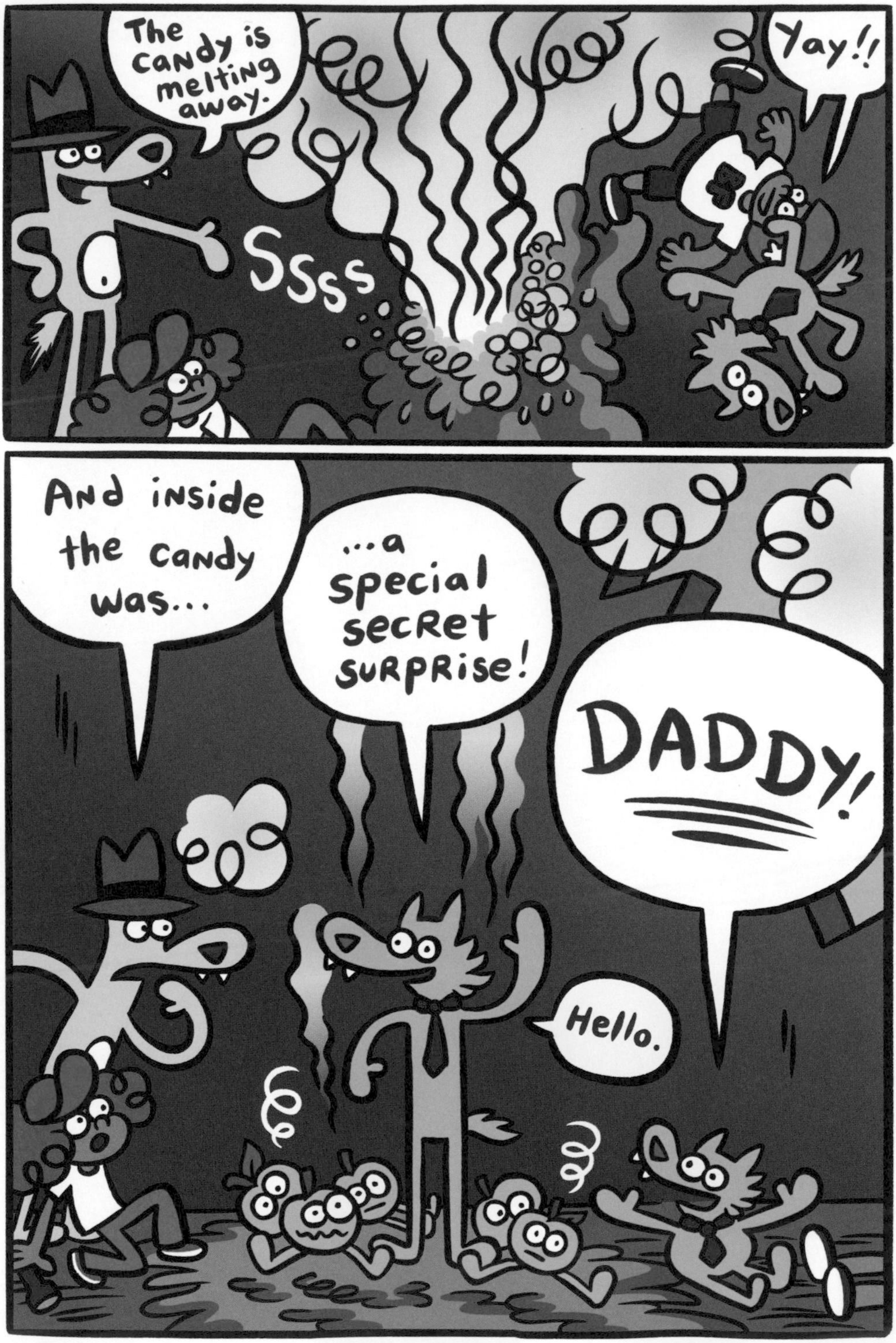
The candy is melting away.
Ssss
Yay!!
And inside the candy was...
...a special secret surprise!
DADDY!
Hello.

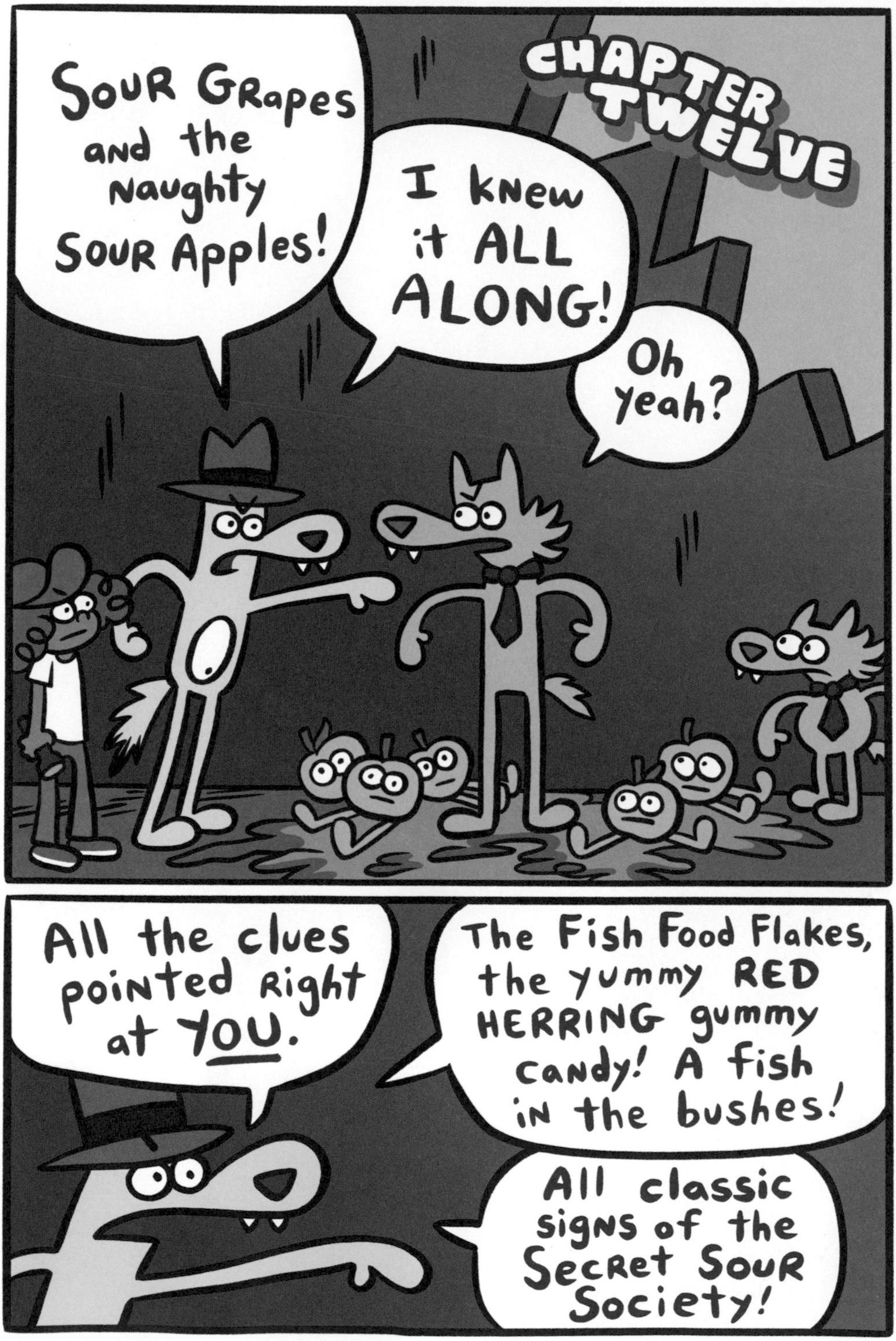
CHAPTER TWELVE
SOUR GRapes and the naughty SOUR Apples!
I knew it ALL ALONG!
Oh yeah?
All the clues pointed Right at YOU.
The Fish Food Flakes, the yummy RED HERRING gummy candy! A fish in the bushes!
All classic signs of the Secret SOUR Society!

64

71